ω

Sign
of the
Carousel

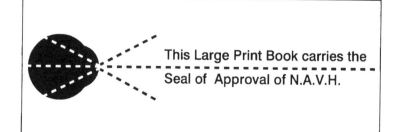

This Large Print Book carries the
Seal of Approval of N.A.V.H.

Sign of the Carousel

Jane Peart

Walker Large Print • Waterville, Maine

Published in 2002 by arrangement with
Natasha Kern Literary Agency, Inc.

The text of this Large Print edition is unabridged.
Other aspects of the book may vary from the original edition.

Set in 16 pt. Plantin by Rick Gundberg.

Printed in the United States on permanent paper.

ISBN 1-4104-0029-8 (lg. print : sc : alk. paper)

To Helene Barnhart,
Teacher and Friend,
For years of supportive encouragement,

Special thanks to:
Mrs. Jaspar Sawatzky
of
"Rose's Antiques"

Chapter One

Stacey Thornton, model-slim in beige slacks and a creamy cashmere sweater, brushed back a strand of honey-blonde hair and took one last look around her San Francisco apartment. Stripped of her personal touches, it stood neatly ready for occupancy by the tenant to whom she was subletting it.

Satisfied that everything was in order, she put on her camel blazer, slung her cordovan leather bag over her shoulder, went out the door, and locked it behind her.

Her excited anticipation of what might lie ahead was mixed with a twinge of nostalgia for what she was leaving. For two years this hillside flat had been her home. It was the longest she had ever lived anywhere except for four years of college. Before that, "home" for Stacey was wherever her Air Force colonel father had been based.

"It's not as if it were forever," she reminded herself as she ran lightly down the steps to where her blue Volkswagen was parked at the curb. "It's only for three months!"

At least, that was what she had told Max, the owner of the small but prestigious art gallery where she worked as his assistant and receptionist. Even Max had been intrigued by the unexpected circumstances that prompted her trip and lent exciting possibilities to Stacey's future plans.

Trinket, her tiny terrier-mix, gave a welcoming bark and a wag of her stubby tail from the passenger's seat as Stacey slipped behind the wheel and started the engine. "Well, we're off on our great adventure, little pal!" she said, and they moved down the steep, winding street.

It was just seven o'clock as they passed through the sleeping neighborhood. Morning mist was drifting over the housetops and the early spring sun was beginning to break through.

By the time she reached the Golden Gate Bridge, its soaring arches and towering spires were glinting in the day's new light. The Bay lay like blue glass on either side. By afternoon it would probably be filled with bobbing boats, their colorful sails billowing in the brisk wind. The day promised to be a glorious one — a typical San Francisco day — Stacey thought with a tiny tug of regret that she would not be there to enjoy it.

"Why?" The puzzled question of her best friend, Kim Spencer, repeated itself in Stacey's mind as she passed the toll cubicles and crossed the bridge. Kim, who had transplanted herself from Arkansas, had become so completely enamored of San Francisco that one would think she had invented the city. She had been stunned at Stacey's announcement.

"Why would anyone want to leave San Francisco?" Kim demanded.

"Why? Would you believe I've just inherited a house and land in Woodfern?" Stacey had replied.

"And where in the world is Woodfern?" asked Kim, totally aghast.

As if reading from a tourist brochure, Stacey told her. "Woodfern is a small, historic town nestled between redwood forests and the ocean in northern California. It used to be a thriving lumber exporting place, years ago, but over the years it has become —"

"Spare me!" Kim had halted the flow of words, holding up her hand. "I still don't understand why you're practically quitting your job, giving up your great apartment, and taking off for somewhere in the boondocks nobody's ever heard of!"

"I'm trying to explain," Stacey had said patiently. "It seems I'm an heiress. My mother's great-aunt has left me her house and land in Woodfern. I'm her namesake. Stacey is a nickname for Eustacia. My aunt was Eustacia Valentine. My mother used to spend summers with her grandmother there when she was a little girl, and I remember her telling us about it when I was growing up. It became a kind of legend, actually . . . you know, everyone's ideal 'hometown.' Maybe that was especially true for our family, moving around as much as we did. Anyway, I guess it took a long time for the will to go through probate, and the lawyers tried to reach me through my parents. But Dad had just been transferred to West Germany and . . . well, it's a long story. I finally got word and decided to go up and take a look at my inheritance."

Kim had speared her with her clear aquamarine eyes. "This wouldn't have anything to do with your breaking up with Todd, would it?" she asked suspiciously.

Stacey shook her head. "No," she said flatly.

Kim regarded her doubtfully. "Seems kind of strange, both things happening about the same time. Quite a coincidence."

Stacey just laughed. Maybe it had been coincidence — divine coincidence, her mother would say. She could almost hear the words

10

again: "What sometimes seems coincidence may be God's way of using circumstances to guide us." But Kim would not have bought that explanation. Kim always thought a man was involved in any decision.

Stacey leaned forward and flipped on the car radio. Ironically, or coincidentally, the music that suddenly flowed out was a sentimental ballad she and Todd had once considered "our song." She switched to another station, not because it made her sad or wistful, only because she was irritated that she had wasted so much time. It seemed incredible to her, now, that she had been taken in by Todd for so long.

They had met one Sunday at the park while both were waiting for a tennis court and hoping for a chance to play. A court had become free and another couple asked them if they wanted to play doubles. Afterward, Todd had insisted on buying her lunch. They had gone to one of her favorite restaurants and sat under the umbrella of a table in the sunlight. The afternoon had suddenly seemed special.

Todd had been flatteringly attentive. He seemed interested to know everything about her — her job, her background, her lifestyle. He admired her hilltop apartment, her casual poise, the way she entertained, the way she dressed.

Stacey had introduced him to her friends, and he had quickly cultivated the ones he felt important. He had pored over her art books, listened to her classical records, quizzed her about the right wines, asked her opinion about the new plays and the bestsellers. She had not realized at first that Todd, new to the city, considered her sophisticated and was awed by her knowledge of things she took for granted — her love of books, ballet, theater, and the fact that she had learned her way around the city.

Growing up as an "Army brat," Stacey had been exposed to a cosmopolitan environment. She had developed, out of necessity because of frequent changes and the expectations of her service-oriented parents, the ability to adapt to new places, different cultures, and varying nationalities and customs. As a young child Stacey had lived in Japan, Belgium, and Germany. She had attended school in five states in America.

Todd came from a rural town in the mid-West that he wanted to forget, and he was anxious to acquire a polish, a veneer that would identify him with the urban world he envied. He fed off Stacey's experience. Too late she had discovered how shallow he was under all his physical attractiveness and glib flattery.

In a way Todd had been just as mistaken about her as she had been about him. After they had been seeing each other for awhile Todd told her his first impression of her. "I thought you might be a model. Brown-eyed blondes are not exactly a dime a dozen. You looked like one of those California girls they always feature in ads and commercials." He had smiled at her — a smile that gave his face enormous charm. It was a practiced smile, Stacey learned, that he used often, well aware of its disarming effect.

"Then, I thought you were a post-debutante from a wealthy family 'playing at a career.' You know, the kind they write about in the society pages of the *Chronicle*."

She had been amused but later realized his comments should have clued her to what Todd was all about. A man who found the social activities of San Francisco's jet set fascinating was looking for something more than Stacey had to offer. As it turned out, she was disillusioned in the end.

Stopped at a traffic light, Stacey mentally shook her head at her own gullibility. She had always believed the best about people, and she had accepted Todd at face value much the same way as she had Trinket when she had found the small creature shivering at her doorstep one rainswept night when she came

13

home from work. She had taken Todd into her life with no question, never suspecting that he used people, then discarded them when they no longer served his purposes. He had used Stacey to gain access to people who could do more for him socially as he moved up the corporate ladder of his company. *Well,* Stacey thought, shrugging, *I can chalk it up to a lesson learned before too much damage was done.*

Actually, it was all for the best. She should have realized from the beginning that Todd was all wrong for her. The expression *not in her game-plan* was one Kim often used, and Stacey used it now but with a difference. Surely Todd was not in God's plan for her. She had been reluctant to admit that when the romance was thriving. Well, she wouldn't make that mistake again!

The sound of a horn being tapped impatiently behind her startled Stacey out of her distraction. She glanced into the rearview mirror and saw a sleek, black sports car. Its driver, a square-jawed man with wheat-colored hair, wind blown and sun streaked, was scowling fiercely behind dark glasses. He had on a roll-necked Irish fisherman's sweater, and looming in back of him was a big, black Labrador.

Trinket immediately scrambled onto the

shelf beneath the rear window of the car and started barking aggressively. She always took on bigger animals when she was safe and secure.

Quickly Stacey shifted gears and moved into the right-hand lane at the first opportunity. The sports car streaked past her. But ironically, at the next intersection the red light halted them both side-by-side, and she could not resist glancing over to see his reaction.

As if aware of her appraising glance, the driver turned, giving her a cool stare. At close range she saw a sun-bronzed face with strong, bluntly handsome features. His eyes were hidden behind the sunglasses, but the expression around his mouth was slightly superior. Stacey felt two simultaneous, yet conflicting sensations — one of attraction, the other of hostility.

When the light changed, his high-powered car shot forward, soon outdistancing Stacey's. Her earlier sensation of antagonism flared ridiculously. To feel such strong emotion toward a perfect stranger seemed idiotic. Maybe it was the whole image he projected — the expensive car, the way he drove it, the arrogant way he held his head — all rankled her. He represented the kind of hedonistic lifestyle she had seen often and come to detest. Her feelings were even stronger when it occurred

15

to her that she knew he was just the sort of person who would have impressed Todd.

The countryside had become increasingly rural and beautiful, and the traffic was negligible. The nearer she came to Woodfern, the more Stacey began to feel the tingling of anticipation.

Every once in a while during the long afternoon, she caught sight of the black sports car, always ahead. But even when they were close, the driver never gave a sign that he recognized her.

It was almost five o'clock when Stacey saw the highway sign indicating the Woodfern exit on the next right. She started to pull over to the right lane, but the black sports car swung in front of her, the dog and his insufferable grin looking back as it passed. Infuriated, Stacey sped up, but the shiny, flashing "rocket" was already making a swift turn onto a lovely multi-arched bridge and disappearing on the road beyond.

Following the same route, Stacey came off the bridge onto a two-lane road that ribboned out between vast expanses of meadowland. To the west lay a line of blue hills against a sunset-streaked sky. A little farther on she saw another sign that gave her heart a little lift: WELCOME TO WOODFERN.

As if she, too, sensed some change in the atmosphere, Trinket roused herself from her basket on the back seat where she had been curled up asleep for the past hour. She placed her forepaws on the front seat and looked about as Stacey entered the main part of town and slowed down to the twenty-five-miles-per-hour speed limit indicated.

"Well, here we are, Trinket!" announced Stacey, feeling a new tremor of excitement.

Woodfern seemed to be one long Main Street with a storybook look. On either side were brightly painted, small, Carpenter's Gothic Victorian houses. Neat gardens, brilliant with flowers, were bordered by intricate fences. As she approached the center of town, she saw little shops of all kinds — an art gallery, a coffee shop, a book store, a dress boutique, and at the end of the street, a restaurant. Across from it stood a bank and a grocery store. As she made a U-turn and started back down the street, she noticed the spires of at least four churches rising above the buildings on the side streets.

Although the lawyers who had handled Aunt Eustacia's estate had written that they would have the house cleaned and aired for her arrival, Stacey knew she would have to stop for food and a few staples and supplies. The Valentine house was a few miles outside the town proper, but from the directions they had given her, it would not be hard to find.

She pulled into the parking lot beside the old-fashioned-looking grocery store. Benches stood outside the double-glass doors of its plain, white-painted front, and baskets of vegetables and fruit were stacked at the entrance. She let Trinket out after fastening on her leash. Then she hooked the loop around the car door, placed a small feeding dish down on the cement, filled it with water from a thermos she carried in the car, and laid two milk bones beside the dish.

"Now, stay, like a good girl. I'll be back as quick as I can," she told the little dog.

Stacey went down the small aisles quickly, filling her basket with coffee, cereal, bread, butter, eggs, chocolate milk, dry dog food, some bananas — enough to tide her over until she had time for a really big shopping trip. At the counter she picked up a local newspaper.

The gray-haired woman clerk who rang up her purchases and the rosy-cheeked boy who bagged her groceries eyed her curiously. But Stacey did not want to explain all about herself yet. There'd be plenty of time to get acquainted. She knew anyone new was always noticed in a town this size. The residents would find out soon enough that the old Valentine house was occupied and that Eustacia's niece had come to live in Woodfern.

Hoisting the bags of groceries into her arms, she started back to the car. But as she left the store she was dismayed to hear the sound of Trinket's frantic barking. She hurried to where her car was parked and immediately saw the reason for Trinket's racket. The sports car with which she had already had several encounters that day was parked alongside her Volkswagen, and the Labrador, every muscle of his body tensed, was glaring down at the small dog. Trinket was lunging and barking at the big animal in a frenzy of aggressiveness. She had become hopelessly entangled in her leash.

As Stacey struggled to untangle Trinket, she became aware of someone behind her. She straightened up, turned around, and found herself face-to-face with her road adversary. She looked directly into two slits of icy blue in a face whose expression was far from friendly.

He was looking at her as if she might just have escaped from somewhere. The look was so unnerving that Stacey was momentarily speechless. With Trinket still yipping at her feet, all she could do was stare at the man's cold annoyance. Finally he spoke, and what he said was even more intimidating.

"When you get your dog under control,

would you please move your vehicle? You're blocking my exit."

Fury surged hotly through Stacey. With clenched teeth she retorted, "As you can plainly see, I am doing my level best to free my poor little animal who is being terrorized by your beast. I will be glad to move my *vehicle* as soon as possible and get out of your way. From what I've observed all day, you and your *vehicle* are a menace on the road."

With that she whirled around and thankfully got the leash straightened out. She lifted the still-squirming Trinket and practically tossed her in the back seat of the car, then slipped behind the wheel. With a minimum of tries she got her engine started, backed out, and turned into the street. Scarcely a minute later, the sports car spun out onto the street and whizzed past her. She pulled over to the side, seething with frustration, gripping the wheel, and stuck out her tongue at the fast disappearing sports car.

Stacey hoped fervently she would never see that impossible man or his car or his dog again.

When she calmed down a little, she realized she had set down her grocery bags and left them in the parking lot when she bent to rescue Trinket. Wearily she turned her car around and drove slowly back to the grocery store.

To her surprise, Stacey saw a petite young woman with a halo of coppery curls standing beside the two abandoned bags of groceries. She wore blue jeans and was holding a baby who looked like a Botticelli cherub.

The woman waved and smiled at Stacey, and came over to speak when she had braked the car and rolled down the window. "Oh, I'm so relieved," she said. "I was afraid you were so upset you'd just drive off forgetting all about your groceries. I was wondering how I'd get them to you." She paused, looking at Stacey sympathetically, and said, "I saw the whole scene as I was coming out of the store."

Stacey looked sheepish. "I guess I said some pretty terrible things, didn't I? But he was such a —" she stopped. "Do you know who that guy is, or better put, who that guy *thinks* he is?"

The girl rolled her eyes expressively. "That is Scott *Lucas*." Her emphasis seemed to explain itself.

"Is that supposed to mean something?" Stacey asked.

"Around here, just about everything. He — that is — the Lucas family owns most of Lucas Valley County, that's the county we live in — Woodfern is part of it. And the Lucases act as if they own Woodfern, too. At least they used to . . . but things are changing

21

— slowly, for sure — but changing."

"I don't think that excuses rudeness," Stacey said stubbornly.

"Neither do I. But then, I've never had a personal confrontation with the gentleman." She smiled sweetly. "By the way, I'm Nora Phillips. This is my son, Brendan, nicknamed Tiger. Obviously you're new in town. Is there anything I can do to help?"

"Thank you. That's awfully nice. I'm Stacey Thornton. I've just come from San Francisco to see some property I've inherited — the Valentine place on Crescent Beach Road."

"You mean that lovely old house?" Nora asked excitedly.

"Yes, do you know it?"

"I pass it every day coming and going from town to home. My husband and I live at Crescent Beach. That's a beautiful house — one of the best examples of Carpenter's Gothic around here. It's gotten a bit run down in the last few years since Miss Valentine's been gone, but . . ." she paused, then rushed on. "I do hope you plan to live there."

"I'm not sure yet. I haven't even seen it. I'm on my way out there now."

The baby wiggled in Nora's arms and she shifted him to her other hip and said, "Well, I better be on my way. He's getting hungry and Jeff will be wondering what's kept us this long." She slid open the door of her van and secured the baby in his car seat. Then she turned and said, "It's really neat you've come here, Stacey. I hope you'll decide to stay. Don't let what happened give you a wrong idea about Woodfern. There are lots of wonderful people here."

Stacey grinned. "Thanks for standing guard over my groceries, Nora."

"Sure, anytime," Nora said with a laugh. "I'll stop by and see how you're getting along in a day or two. Good-bye for now, and good luck!" she called out as she got in the van and drove away with a cheerful wave.

Nora's wish echoed in Stacey's mind as she drove out the beach road and as she slowed to read the faded lettering on a rusted mailbox perched precariously on a listing wooden post. "E. Valentine" it read. With a sinking heart Stacey peered through the gathering dusk up a rutted driveway overgrown with shaggy bushes. At the end of it, its peaked roof piercing the darkening sky, Stacey saw a tall, shabby, gray wood-frame house.

Was this what she had inherited?

" 'Good luck' indeed," she repeated to herself. It certainly looked as though she was going to need it. A lot.

Chapter Two

Stacey turned into the driveway and inched around its curve, then came to a stop in front of the house. She opened the car door to let Trinket scamper out while she sat staring at her inheritance with the growing conviction that she had made a terrible mistake. She had left her job and her apartment to come nearly three hundred miles to this.

She got out of the car, finally, and stood looking up at the tall building, her eyes following the three tiers of porches that seemed to go all around. In the approaching gloom of evening, the house seemed dark and brooding with its high, heavy roof, hooded gables, and intricately carved arches. Edging the gaunt structure were elaborate, cut-out trimmings of wooden lace that looked for all the world like old-fashioned paper valentines. The name she had called it, the Valentine house, seemed oddly appropriate.

Stacey groped in her handbag for the ring of

keys she had been sent by the lawyers who handled her aunt's estate. Whatever she had let herself in for, she was here now and there was nothing else to do but go inside.

She whistled for Trinket and started up the porch steps, each one sagging and creaking under her foot. The front door was a double one with etched glass windows in the upper half. Stacey inserted the key in the lock, turned it, and it opened with a protesting squeak. Inside, there was the slight musty odor of a house long closed. But as Stacey found a light switch and snapped it on to illuminate the dim interior of the entry hall, she saw a staircase with a handsomely carved newel post and balustrade leading to the second floor. The light was coming from a beautiful prismed chandelier hanging from the tall ceiling.

She was too tired from her long trip and the excitement to make a complete inspection of the house that evening. She was trying her best to quell the stirrings of panic and to recover her usually optimistic nature as she faced the facts of her "inheritance." Obviously the house was too big, too crammed with furniture, had too many tall windows in too many rooms, and the grounds were a wilderness. But what she was going to do about it all, she decided, like the legendary Scarlett

O'Hara, she would decide "tomorrow."

She found the kitchen and to her relief saw that it had been modernized within the last ten years. She fed Trinket, then heated herself a can of soup, opened the box of crackers, and made herself some tea.

She suddenly felt weary beyond belief. A good night's sleep would make everything look different, she told herself.

A small, iron wood stove stood in the kitchen with a box of neatly stacked wood beside it. She had no trouble getting a fire lighted, and soon the chill of the long-empty house had vanished. Stacey sipped her tea, her mind too tired to come to any conclusions. Trinket had settled into her basket with a sigh and seemed to have made herself at home. Of course, anywhere with Stacey would be "home" for Trinket.

Adjoining the kitchen was a small room that had probably been called the "family parlor" as opposed to the larger, formal "company parlor" in the front of the house. Stacey placed her sleeping bag on the curved back sofa, telling herself it would be warmer down here than in one of the upper bedrooms.

Through the windows she could occasionally see the moving lights of a car or truck passing on the road, but nothing else broke the dense darkness of the country night. Used to the sounds of the city, Stacey felt very isolated. If she had not been so bone-tired, she might have found it hard to get to sleep.

Just before she drifted off, she heard the click of Trinket's paws on the linoleum floor of the kitchen as she covered the short distance from her basket to the foot of the sofa. Stacey felt a soft plop as Trinket jumped up, circled twice, then settled down on Stacey's feet.

Stacey stirred and was instantly wide awake. The room was full of light and had lost the shadowy gloom of the night. She got out of her sleeping bag and put a few more small pieces of wood into the stove, filled a blue enameled kettle with water, and set it on the burner to boil.

Although the room was large and had high ceilings, it had the coziness of a farm family kitchen. It was furnished with a big, round oak table, spindle chairs with pressed wood backs, and a pine hutch filled with Willowware.

After she had made herself some instant coffee, Stacey explored the main floor. Carrying her mug with her, she looked into every room. There were eight, all crowded with handsome Victorian furniture that was dark, ornate, and of beautiful wood. It

27

seemed more and more furniture had been pushed into each room without ever removing any to make space for additional pieces.

Back in the huge center hall, Stacey gazed up the stairway to the second floor. There was a gorgeous stained glass window on the landing, and now, as the sun began to shine, a lovely rainbow of colored light streamed in. In that light, the interior of the house looked less formidable. It was a gracious remnant of another era, almost intact.

She walked into one of the twin parlors that flanked the front door and opened the inside shutters of the bay window, letting the sunlight flood the room. From there she looked out on what must have once been a glorious garden. Through the tangle of rose bushes gone wild and rhododendron as large as small trees, she could see an ornamental birdbath and what appeared to be a sculptured Grecian figure of a small child beside what could be a fountain or goldfish pond.

Along the drive on either side were maple trees that would be red and gold in fall. The bushes just under the window might be lilacs with fragrant plumes in June.

Little by little the oppressive feeling Stacey had felt the night before began to lift. Of course, it would take lots of work but this place could be . . .

Her practical thoughts stemmed her imagination. She let it go no further. It was still too soon to make any plans. But nonetheless she felt happy — happier, she realized, than she had felt in months.

As she stood basking in the sunlight and her new euphoria, to her amazement, Stacey saw a silver Mercedes turn into the driveway and approach the house. She ran to the back of the house, but before she could dress, the shrill ring of the twist doorbell sounded. Stacey grabbed her robe, flung it on, and hurried to the front door.

The woman standing on the porch was large, her leathery face lined and coarse-skinned. Her hair stood like a salt and pepper halo around her head. Her eyes were alert and intelligent and she had a wide, friendly smile as she greeted Stacey.

"Good morning! I saw lights here last night and I couldn't resist stopping to see who'd moved in. I'm on my way back to the city and even though I know I should have waited a decent length of time to let you get settled before popping in on you . . . well, that's how I am. Curiosity's one of my many faults."

Her rapid-fire monologue gave Stacey time to observe the woman's expensive soft tweed suit, her good leather bag and boots, the gold necklace against a Shetland sweater, and the flash of a large diamond ring on her rather red, rough hands. As it seemed the natural next step, Stacey introduced herself. Then so did her visitor.

"I'm Leta Townsend — used to be Leta Russell. Both my husband's family and mine are old-timers in Woodfern. We're forced to live in San Francisco now because of Fred's work, but I get up here at least every other weekend. I still own some property and keep horses to ride." She paused, as if suddenly aware that Stacey had not said anything yet, and that she was shivering in the cool morning wind.

"Oh, say! I got you up, didn't I? Sorry. I get up and ride at dawn when I'm up here. My horses need exercising badly. They're getting saddle shy . . . but what I came by for was —" She looked a little abashed, then proceeded. "I've always wanted to see the inside of this house. Miss Valentine was rather a recluse for years, you know. Then after she died, it was closed up. Would you mind if I came in and took a look around?"

Confronted with such self-confidence, Stacey could not think of any reason to refuse, so she stepped back and motioned Leta Townsend inside.

The older woman looked around and gave a long, low whistle.

"I knew it," she remarked almost to herself. "This place is a gold mine of antiques. Do you have any idea what a dealer in San Francisco would give for a third of what's here?"

Stacey followed her as she moved first to the door of the large front parlor, then across the hall where sliding doors opened into a huge dining room. Leta drew in her breath and pointed out a piece to Stacey. "Take that Waterford chandelier. The center has deep purple Bristol glass and crystal prisms, and look at the china cabinet, a fortune in cut-glass." She turned and looked at Stacey sharply. "What do you plan to do with all this?"

"I — I haven't any real plans. I just got here last night. I guess I plan to live here," she stammered.

Leta pursed her lips, squinted her eyes, and seemed to be making a quick evaluation.

"If you've got a cup of coffee to spare, I'll tell you what I'd do if I were in your shoes."

"Come into the kitchen. I have water boiling, but the coffee is instant," Stacey offered hesitantly.

"That'll do just fine," Leta said briskly.

The fire in the wood stove was crackling, and the blue enameled kettle was steaming. Stacey found another mug, put out the jar of instant coffee, poured milk from a carton into

31

a pitcher, and placed it on the table. Leta was examining a plate from the hutch when Stacey filled their mugs with boiling water. Then she sat down at the table with her strange, unexpected caller.

"It looks to me as if you've walked into a windfall, young lady. I don't know what your background or experience is, but I figure you to be smart enough to know a good thing when you see it and take some good advice. First, I'd better give you my credentials. The Townsends are one of a few pioneer families who settled in this part of northern California, bought up most of the land, and prospered.

"I married into the family and inherited two housefuls of valuable antiques through my husband. So I know what I'm talking about. I've also shopped around enough antique stores in the Bay area to know not only how much my own things are worth — although most of the stores down there are way over-priced — but I can also see the pieces Miss Valentine had are excellent and in fine condition."

Leta stirred her coffee thoughtfully for a full minute and then declared vigorously, "So, you know what I'd do if I were you? I'd open an antique store. Right here. There's plenty of space for a show room. You could open up the two front rooms — the large parlor and the dining room. That way you'd have the back part of the house for your own living quarters and still have room to spare. What about the upstairs? I bet there are at least six rooms with complete bedroom sets up there." Leta made a broad sweeping gesture. "You could sell half of what's crammed in here and still have enough to furnish an eight-room house."

"But I don't know anything about the antique business," protested Stacey mildly.

"You can read up on it. Woodfern has a good library. You're smart and young enough to learn." Leta finished her coffee and stood up. "What else can you do with this house . . . if you expect to live here? You did come to stay, didn't you?"

"I've sort of burned my bridges behind me," Stacey admitted.

"It takes a special kind of person to like living in a remote area like this," Leta said shrewdly. "Some people who're born here can't wait to get away, my husband, for example. Oh, he enjoys coming up here for weekends or for a week or two in the spring and fall, but he dislikes the natural limits of a small town. Now me, I love it. We'll probably come back here when he retires. There's a lot going on now in Woodfern, new things. I like what I see happening in the town . . . although there

33

are some who don't. Some people can't stand change — any change. But, just as in breeding horses, a town needs new blood every once in a while. Why, Woodfern's come alive in the last few years. Well, I'd best be on my way." Leta started moving toward the hall.

"I hope you think seriously about what I've suggested. Mark my words, it's the answer. Not only would you turn a nice profit, I'm sure, but it would give you an investment in the town, a place in the community, and that's important. . . ."

Stacey followed her guest to the front door where Leta asked her abruptly, "Do you ride?"

Stacey nodded. "I used to ride the bridle trails in Golden Gate Park once or twice a month in good weather."

"You're welcome to ride any of ours you'd like. They need regular exercising, and Pete, our caretaker, would be glad for help in doing it. They get too wild and ornery if they're allowed to run in the pasture all the time. They forget they're meant to be ridden."

Leta slapped her leather gloves against her purse. "Well, so long, Miss Stacey Thornton. I wish you the best, and I'd like to see you start a business here. I'm sure you'd make a go of it."

What a character! Stacey thought to herself

as she watched the silver Mercedes drive off. Leta's visit had lasted no more than a half-hour, but her impact lingered. The suggestion she had made seemed unrealistic. But then, maybe it wasn't. Stacey looked around the house again, this time taking inventory in each room. An antique business? Maybe Leta had a good idea. Upstairs, just as she had predicted, were six bedrooms, each with dark, massively carved, ornate Victorian furnishings. Stacey didn't personally like some of it, but she knew that Leta was correct. They would be priceless in today's inflated market, especially so because, as Leta had keenly surmised, most of the pieces had probably been moved in when the house was new and scarcely used since.

Leta was also right about Stacey's living here. What was she going to do if she stayed in Woodfern? She had come to satisfy her curiosity about her unexpected inheritance. The thought had crossed her mind, after her first sight of the huge house and six acres, that she should probably see a realtor and put it on the market to sell. She had even fantasized that with the money she would take a cruise, even a trip around the world. Then what? What would she have after that?

But if she had her own business — an antique business — it might really be an inheritance that would go on and on. Maybe what Great-Aunt Eustacia had bequeathed her was a whole new life.

A new beginning, a fresh start — wasn't that what, subconsciously, she had been seeking when she left San Francisco? Maybe, just maybe, what her mother believed about divine coincidence was what she believed, too. A ripple of excitement zinged through Stacey.

First things first, the practical part of her directed. She needed to see just what her inheritance consisted of, for she really had no idea what the rest of the house contained.

Stacey hurriedly dressed, pulling on old jeans and a ribbed turtleneck sweater, and began some serious exploring. The rest of the morning she went through the entire house, looking at everything with new eyes. She began to see what Leta Townsend saw, a treasure-trove ripe for her to harvest.

At the end of the second-floor hallway, a door led up another flight of steps to the attic. Stacey, who had always lived in modern houses, had forgotten that all old houses had attics. This one ran the whole length of the house.

Under the slanting ceiling were numerous alcoves set with dormer windows through which the late morning sun revealed an overwhelming array. Stacey looked about with bewildered dismay. She had never seen such masses of stuff! Among old trunks, boxes, and cartons packed with who knew what, was more furniture — dressers, bedsteads, chairs, rockers, bureaus — all wedged tightly together in endless rows.

Stunned with the enormity of the task of taking any kind of inventory, Stacey just stood there for a few minutes, the dust of the years tickling her nostrils, wondering where to begin.

Then in a far corner she spotted the merry-go-round horse and walked over to it. It must have been on a small carousel, perhaps placed in the yard years ago for the Valentine children.

Stacey found an old rag-filled box and took a scrap of cloth. She dusted the horse off affectionately, hearing in her own mind the distant sound of calliope music she always associated with happy childhood memories. With her hand she lightly caressed the curve of the horse's neck. She touched the flowing mane, admiring the proud lift of the head and the once brightly painted, but now tarnished, gold-and-red bridle and saddle.

A prickling along her scalp and a curious sort of elation quickened inside her. If, by the wildest chance, she did decide to take Leta Townsend's suggestion and open an antique store, wouldn't this be the perfect symbol for it? She could almost see a wooden sign swinging over it at the end of the driveway reading, "ANTIQUES AT THE SIGN OF THE CAROUSEL."

Chapter Three

"At the Sign of the Carousel!" Nora repeated slowly. "I like it! I really do! And I think it's a fantastic idea!"

Nora Phillips had arrived the following afternoon with a covered casserole for Stacey to stick in the oven for supper so she wouldn't have to bother cooking while she got settled.

Touched by this neighborly gesture, Stacey had invited Nora in for tea and to test the idea Leta Townsend had planted on her.

Nora's immediate enthusiasm sparked Stacey's own, and after she took Nora on a tour of the house, they were sitting at the kitchen table talking a mile a minute.

"Of course, it's probably crazy," commented Stacey, cautiously hoping Nora would contradict her but afraid of runaway impulsiveness. "It can't be as simple as hanging out a sign. I'll have to research the antique business, then get a business license, and probably go before the city council. It gets pretty complicated, actually."

"Yes, I know. We investigated it when we first moved here. Jeff and I were thinking about opening a store to sell his pottery. There was so much red tape involved. But that wasn't the real reason we didn't open a store in Woodfern. Jeff likes going to the craft shows, not having to keep regular business hours, creating what he wants to make, and selling it rather than doing things to order and putting up with the hassle of running a business."

"Well, I guess one of the first things I have to do is learn what's the first thing to do!" Stacey said, laughing. "It's kind of exciting, but scary, too."

"I think it's a great idea, and I'm sure you'll work it all out," Nora assured her. "I have a real sense about things like that."

"What are you — a psychic or something?" Stacey teased.

"Sort of — like right now — I predict you are about to have an unexpected visitation." Nora's big eyes widened as her glance went past Stacey's shoulder out the window.

Puzzled, Stacey turned and looked in the same direction just in time to see Scott Lucas get out of his sports car, slam the door behind him, and stride purposefully to the porch. He was not smiling.

"I don't think that's the Woodfern Welcome Wagon!" said Nora with raised eyebrows.

The shrill sound of the doorbell being twisted impatiently echoed through the house. Exchanging perplexed looks and shrugs with Nora, Stacey got up and started down the hall to the front door. Just as she opened it, the bell shrilled again.

The stunned expression on Scott Lucas's face at seeing Stacey seemed frozen there for a full minute. Then it was replaced by a fierce frown.

He was wearing a wide-brimmed cowboy hat that tipped back from his forehead. His thumbs hooked into a leather belt on well-worn jeans and his Western-style wool shirt made Scott Lucas look perfectly typecast for a hero in one of those TV "sagebrush" dramas. Stacey almost smiled at the idea, but the coldness of those intense blue eyes staring at her from his deeply tanned face stopped any amusement.

Remembering his articulate scolding at their last meeting, she felt a sudden perverse pleasure in his speechlessness. But at his first words, indignation rushed up inside her.

"I didn't know this property was for sale. If I had, I would have bought it," he said shortly.

"It wasn't for sale. It isn't. I own the house and I am going to live here."

He flushed under his tan, and his mouth tightened. "I understood it was tied up in an unsettled estate."

"Well, it was settled, and I inherited it."

"Are you a Valentine?" he demanded.

"I'm Stacey Thornton. Miss Eustacia Valentine was my mother's aunt. She left the house and property to me."

His frown deepened. "I was told it was willed to a distant relative who would be willing to sell."

"Well, whoever told you that was wrong." Stacey started to close the door. But Scott Lucas held up his hand to halt her.

"I am very interested in this property. I'm willing to make you a generous offer. You could make a quick sale at a good profit," he said.

"I'm not interested in making a quick sale. I told you —"

"Not even at an enormous profit?" he interrupted, lifting his eyebrows skeptically. With that he gave a scornful jerk of his head toward her small, dusty car then looked back at her, giving her a long, slow once-over. Stacey felt her face grow warm, knowing he was taking in her faded jogging outfit of baggy sweatshirt and pants and old running shoes. As if esti-

42

mating her net worth by her appearance was not enough, he said, "This place is in bad shape! It needs everything from new rain gutters to a total overhaul. That takes a lot of money."

He ended his statement with a slight but implicit assumption that she did not have that kind of money. Stacey found the remark not only infuriating, but also presumptuous and rudely insinuating. She drew herself up in stony fury.

He took advantage of her temporary loss of words.

"May I?" he said and before she could protest he had walked past her and into the hall. He looked around, then gave her a direct glance, meant to be intimidating, she was sure. With a knowing smile, he said condescendingly, "Oh, come on now. Why would a young woman from the city want to live way out in this isolated country house alone?" He then fixed her with a cold smile. "Maybe you're playing a little game to gain an even higher offer? Has someone already made one? I'll meet whatever you've been offered."

"I repeat it is *not* for sale," Stacey said evenly, holding herself rigid.

"You certainly don't intend to farm the land, nor raise cattle, nor graze sheep!" His voice was heavy with sarcasm. "So what on earth are you going to do with all the land around this house?"

"I really don't see how any of this concerns you or that it is any of your business what I intend to do!" Stacey burst out angrily, losing her control.

"Do you know who I am?" he asked fiercely.

"Yes, even though you didn't have the manners to introduce yourself!" she retorted. "And if it is true that you and your family own half this county, why would you want a mere six acres more?"

"Never mind why. I do want it."

"That's nothing to me!" Stacey's color was high. It took a strong effort to keep her inner anger from showing. "I don't know how to make it any clearer, Mr. Lucas, but I have no intention of selling either the house or the land."

His eyes were like blue fire as he snapped, "I'll get the appraiser's value and double it."

"You don't seem to understand. It is *not* for sale."

The silence that followed crackled with tension; then Scott Lucas took a couple of long strides back to the door. With his hand on the knob, he turned to Stacey and said, "You may know my name, Miss Thornton, but you don't know *me*. When I want something, I

44

usually get it . . . whether it be a piece of land, a horse or . . ."

Here he paused and Stacey cut in hotly. "Well, don't count on it this time, Mr. Lucas. Your luck may have just run out!"

Something curious flickered in his eyes for a moment and he gave her a look that she was too angry to analyze. Then, without another word he turned, walked out the door and down the steps, the sound of his boots clattering on the wood.

Seething, Stacey watched him get in his car and back out of the driveway with a roar. He spun his tires at the end and tore down the road.

Behind her she heard Nora voice a soft "Wow!" and she turned to see her standing wide-eyed in the kitchen doorway. "I always heard Scott Lucas had a temper, but I've never seen him in action before!"

Stacey was shaking as she walked back to the kitchen.

"And you stood right up to him, Stacey," Nora said admiringly, pouring Stacey a fresh cup of hot tea.

Stacey sank into the chair opposite her. Her knees felt weak. After only two days in Woodfern, she had had two encounters which had revealed a part of her personality she had only been dimly aware of before.

"I was really proud of you." Nora smiled encouragingly.

Stacey shook her head doubtfully. "I surprised myself," she said.

"Well, he certainly had it coming," Nora said philosophically.

But Stacey wasn't so sure. Within two days she had turned a handsome stranger into an enemy. And if what she'd heard about Scott Lucas was true, he was a powerful enemy.

Chapter Four

The terms of Aunt Eustacia's will had been simple and plain. Stacey thought she had understood them. She was to inherit everything — the house, its furnishings, and the six acres surrounding it. They were hers to use or dispose of in any way she chose. There were no stipulations that she could read even in the small print.

But after Scott Lucas's threatening call, she decided to go into Woodfern and see Aunt Eustacia's lawyers, the executors of her will. In their formal letter to Stacey before she left San Francisco they had encouraged her to contact them as was "convenient" after her arrival in Woodfern, stating that they would welcome any opportunity to be of service.

As Stacey drove the four miles into town, she enjoyed the picturesque countryside on either side of the two-lane road. The fields were yellow with mustard, placid cows grazed serenely in the green pastureland, and beyond them the rim of blue hills rose to meet the sky. What a change it was from the glass and concrete of the city!

Entering the town of Woodfern, Stacey was reminded of a New England village, where her father had been stationed at Westover Field, and of the summers they had spent on Cape Cod. Main Street, with its quaint Victorian storefronts and the spires of white, wood-frame churches reaching upward, seemed oddly out of place in California.

She found a parking place easily, and since the letterhead of the attorneys' stationery bore the address "Main Street," Stacey knew she would have no trouble locating the office. Main Street was only about four blocks long.

The entrance to the law offices was a door in the recessed foyer of a rather shabby building at one end of Main Street, marked by a brass plaque in need of polishing. It read, "Whitlow & Meade, Attorneys at Law."

The office itself was also rather shabby looking, and no one was sitting at the reception desk in the outer office when Stacey opened the door. A worn, leather sofa and a matching armchair stood to one side of another door, presumably leading to an inner office, labeled with peeling gold letters, "PRIVATE."

She stood uncertainly for a moment, wondering what she should do to announce her presence. While she was still trying to decide whether to knock, clear her throat loudly, or call out "Hello," the door opened and a young man with a shock of sandy-colored hair and horn-rimmed glasses peered out.

"Good morning!" he greeted Stacey cheerfully. "Can I help you?"

Stacey hesitated slightly. He looked almost too boyish to be a lawyer. "Mr. Whitlow?" she asked tentatively.

"Nope. Meade. Larry Meade." He came out, extending his hand. "Mr. Whitlow was my father's partner, now retired. My dad's Lawrence Meade. I'm new in the firm, but I'm gradually taking over some of Dad's clients. He was Miss Eustacia Valentine's lawyer. Welcome to Woodfern, Miss Thornton."

Stacey, used to the anonymity of the city, was totally taken back by this instant recognition. "How did you know?" she gasped.

Larry Meade's grin broadened as his eyes swept admiringly over the willowy blonde in the softly tailored teal blue suit. Her classic navy pumps showed off her slender ankles, and she was carrying a handsome leather bag. Everything about her said city, not small town. Stacey Thornton may have inherited Miss Valentine's fortune, but style wasn't something one inherited.

Suppressing a chuckle at the question, Larry Meade just shook his head and explained. "In a place this size any stranger is noticed. Anyway, we've been expecting you. You did write and tell us you'd be here around the first. Won't you come in my office where we can talk?" He stood aside and held the door open for her to walk through.

"Coffee?" he asked, once she was seated across a square, rather battered table that served as his desk.

Stacey accepted the mug he poured for her from a battered percolator on the hot plate behind him. "I came this morning because I wanted to make sure that everything was in order about my aunt's will. I mean, there aren't any liens against the estate or anything that might put my owning the house and property in jeopardy?"

Larry threw out his hands in an open gesture.

"Nothing that I know of, Miss Thornton. Dad wrote the will according to Miss Eustacia's explicit instructions and went over it with a proverbial fine-toothed comb. Everything is in perfect legal order. Why? Do you have some problem with it?"

"No, it's just that — well, I heard that it might have been mistakenly considered for sale."

"Well, there may have been a rumor to that effect when it took so long to locate you, the heir, because of your father being overseas . . . but no other reason I can think of." He paused. "Are you thinking of selling?"

Stacey took a sip of coffee. It was lukewarm and bitter, and she set the mug down. Larry followed suit, then grimaced and said apologetically. "Whew! That's awful. I just heated what was left over from yesterday when I came in this morning. I'll make some more!"

"No, please don't bother, at least not for me," Stacey told him. "I've got to be going. I just wanted to make sure everything about my inheritance was settled." She picked up her purse and stood.

Larry unfolded his lanky frame and rose also.

"There was a little difficulty about the taxes a few years ago . . ." he said. "You know, Miss Eustacia was a pacifist and she withheld her income taxes for some time, but my father liquidated some old, valuable stock she had and took care of the IRS so there would be no claim against the property from the government." Larry Meade came around to Stacey's side and said reassuringly, "No, siree, Miss Thornton, you don't have a thing to worry about as far as owning the house and land. You are going to stay in Woodfern, then?"

Stacey waited a moment before answering. "Actually, I'm thinking — just thinking — of going into business here. The antique business. The house is full of more furniture than I could ever possibly use, and I understand it is all quite valuable."

Larry Meade looked surprised. "We all thought — I mean, my father and I discussed the fact that you'd probably want to look the property over, but we never thought — I mean you being from the city —" He stopped as if embarrassed that he'd said too much. But his curiosity got the best of him and he blurted out. "Why does a city girl want to open an antique store in a remote little town on the North Coast?"

Stacey laughed lightly. "I said I was just thinking about it. But does the idea sound so outlandish?"

"Well, you're a city girl, and this is such an out-of-the-way place. Won't you miss the bright lights and all that?"

"Please don't label me so quickly! It's my theory that a person can adjust to anything — climate, situation, country — given time. I know. I've done it." She smiled at him to take some of the sharpness from her tone. "Granted, some people need more time than others. But I think I'll get used to it very quickly. In fact, I think I'm going to love Woodfern."

Larry Meade opened the office door for her and walked with her out to the front room.

"It may seem great to you now. It's nearly spring and it's real pretty here from now on through the summer. But I'm not sure you're prepared for our long coastal winters . . . the rain, fog, and winds can get very depressing," he said doubtfully.

"You forget I've lived in San Francisco," Stacey assured him. "Fog is no stranger to me."

"Well, good luck, Miss Thornton, whatever you decide. And if you need any help, please feel free to come by. Anytime!"

"Thank you. I certainly will." She started out the door when she was halted by Larry Meade's afterthought question.

"Oh, by the way, who told you that the property might be for sale?"

"A Mr. Scott Lucas." She turned to watch Larry Meade's reaction with interest.

"Scott, huh?" He nodded slowly as if not surprised. "He didn't waste any time getting to you then."

"You know him?" she asked.

"Everyone knows Scott Lucas," he replied. "Sure, we went to school together until he was sent off to a fancy prep school when the rest of us started high school. Then he went to Cal Tech. His father wanted him to learn everything he could about the ranching business. After college I went to law school, so we didn't see much of each other during those years."

"He's quite a determined man," Stacey commented dryly.

"Yes, well, all the Lucases tend to throw their weight around somewhat. Prestige and power mean a lot, and in this community the Lucases have both."

Stacey's natural curiosity about Scott Lucas was piqued but not wanting to appear eager for gossip, she said good-bye to Larry and left.

Just as she was nearly at her car she saw a yellow Jeep zooming down Main Street, and at its wheel was the man she had just been discussing with Larry. Stacey had the urge to duck into the nearest store, but she was not quick enough. Scott Lucas had spotted her. He swerved his vehicle into an empty parking space, jumped out of it, and came striding toward her.

As he came closer, his blazing eyes riveted upon her, paralyzing movement. Then to her complete astonishment his expression changed into a friendly smile, full of warmth and openness.

"Miss Thornton." He stood in front of her, cutting off any possibility of escape. He looked down at her from his six-foot-plus height with a confident nonchalance. "We got off on rather a bad foot the other morning. I'm really sorry about that. It's just that I've had my eye on that particular property for quite a while and understood it was only a matter of untangling some legal red tape before it would be available. I guess my disappointment outweighed my good manners. It probably gave you the wrong impression of me. I'm not usually quite so . . . ." he gave a short laugh. "At any rate, why don't we go and have a cup of coffee and talk? I feel sure we can reach a mutually satisfactory agreement. If it's a matter of price . . . ."

"I thought I made it clear yesterday, Mr. Lucas. I am not at all interested in selling the property. And price is not the issue," Stacey said evenly with all the dignity she could muster.

Scott's face flushed a deep red under the bronze skin, and his mouth tightened as he struggled to keep his temper.

"But why in the world are you holding out? A city girl like you can have no legitimate use for an old country house and barn and six acres of prime pastureland!"

"You're wrong! I have a very legitimate use for it. I'm opening an antique store and I'm going to live there, too, and for the last time, none of it is for sale!" Stacey burst out.

Lucas seemed stunned at her vehemence, and his face registered angry disbelief.

Trembling with fury, Stacey brushed by him and hurried to her car. Her hand was shaking as she pushed the key in the ignition, but she started the VW without stalling and drove off.

Halfway down the beach road to her house she realized the abrasive encounter with Scott Lucas had distracted her so much she had not completed her other errands. Worse still, he had pressured her into the announcement that she was going into business before she herself had even decided to do it!

Stacey ground her teeth! That insufferable man! Now she would have to stay in Woodfern and open an antique store!

Chapter Five

Stacey had been invited by Nora to supper on Saturday evening and given a map to the hilltop house and pottery shop. As Stacey followed the drawing a little after six-thirty, she wondered what Nora would say when she told her about running into Scott Lucas and blurting out her uncompleted plans so recklessly.

And it had been reckless, a statement certainly made under duress and not legally binding, she reassured herself.

"Pride goeth before a fall" the biblical admonition drummed warningly in Stacey's head. Pride or no pride she felt she had to take Leta's advice and at least try the antique business, even if it were only to show him. Him? Who? *Scott Lucas, of course!* Her own answer made her feel rather foolish. *Why should you care?* She mentally shrugged and quoted another proverb "Having put your hand to the plow, do not turn back." It was full speed ahead now. She was determined.

Ahead on the left she saw the sign Nora had told her to look for: "Potter's Field." "My husband Jeff's weird sense of humor," Nora had explained.

She shifted into low gear as the little car ground up the rutted hillside to where Jeff and Nora Phillips's home clung to the cliffs overlooking the ocean.

The cottage, with its weathered shingles and slanting roof, looked small, cozy, and friendly. The blue Dutch door stood open to the sunshine, and bright geraniums in clay pots were clustered on the small stone apron. The surrounding meadow was purple and gold with wild lupin and California poppies.

A building stood beyond the house that Stacey assumed was Jeff's workshop and kiln. Two other cars were parked in the clearing beside the house — a Dodge station wagon and an old but shiny Austin Mini. Nora had told Stacey some other guests were invited — friends she wanted her to meet.

Nora appeared at the doorway as Stacey got out of the car. She was wearing a long, embroidered skirt and a top that made her gray-green eyes appear turquoise. She greeted Stacey warmly and led her inside.

The interior of the cottage reflected Nora's creative charm with its painted wood pieces and vintage wicker furniture piled with patch-work pillows in bright colors.

"Neil and Aris Brady are already here," Nora said as she took Stacey through the hallway to the entrance of the low-ceilinged living room. "Neil owns the bookstore in town."

A slightly built man with thick, wavy, gray hair and a fine, sensitive face stood as they came in and gave Stacey a firm handshake at Nora's introduction. His wife, Aris, a middle-aged woman, greeted Stacey with a pleasant smile and twinkling blue eyes behind Ben Franklin glasses.

"Fay is out with Jeff in the workshop admiring his new glaze," Nora explained. "They should be in shortly, although you never know with two artists! Fay paints huge acrylics, which you won't believe when you see her size."

"Are Shawn and Val coming?" Neil asked.

"Yes, but they'll probably be late," Nora warned with a little laugh. "You know Val will have to decide on her costume."

"And, of course, make her entrance," added Aris chuckling.

Neither remark, Stacey noticed, was mean or sarcastic. The comments were given as though discussing a beloved child.

Nora turned to Stacey as she handed her a glass of icy apple cider. "Val is our resident 'star.' She and her husband manage the Woodfern Repertory Theater. Shawn directs, and Val is an actress. Together they've put on some great performances in very limited facilities."

"The Woodfern Little Theater is gaining a real reputation," Neil said.

"Maybe we'll be rivaling Ashland one day," suggested Aris, referring to Oregon's Shakespeare center.

The next person to arrive was Florin Mickloff, owner of the local art gallery, a slender young man with a beard and deep-set eyes.

"You two should have a lot in common," Nora said as she introduced them. "Stacey used to work at a San Francisco gallery."

Just then the back door opened and the sound of voices drifted into the room.

"Here come Jeff and Fay now!" announced Nora happily as a tall, thin young man and a tiny woman with a halo of frizzy, grayish-red hair entered the room.

"Hi, you two. I want you to meet Stacey Thornton."

Fay fluttered forward. "How nice to meet you. Nora's given you high marks, so I hope we'll be friends too. You must come to my studio soon."

Jeff Phillips nodded his head shyly in

Stacey's direction. His brown curly hair was rather long and accented his kind hazel eyes. He would take some time to get to know, Stacey thought. But as she watched him swing little Brendan, who ran to him, up in his arms it was plain to see father and son adored each other. Jeff's friendship would be worth cultivating, Stacey concluded.

Just then the Kents arrived in a flurry. Val, attired in a colorful, flowing caftan, acknowledged her introduction to Stacey by extending both hands and greeting her with dramatic flare.

"How marvelous, darling!" she said in a deep, fluid voice.

Shawn, in a navy blazer, gray flannels, and an ascot tie knotted at his neck, looked like a perennial leading man himself and gave Stacey a brief, continental-style bow.

As they sipped the cider Nora served, the conversation flowed with ease and was punctuated with laughter. Stacey could tell these people were not only comfortable with each other but also with themselves. She couldn't help comparing this gathering with the artificiality and forced conviviality she had experienced at some San Francisco parties.

When they assembled around the round dinner table set with Jeff's pottery and a centerpiece of wild flowers, they all held hands unself-consciously while Jeff offered a simple grace. This unpretentious gesture touched Stacey. She had not been any place for a meal where a blessing was said since she had left home.

Nora brought out a big tureen from which she ladled a savory stew that smelled of herbs and dark gravy, thick with beef and garden vegetables. A basket of crusty, rough-textured, homemade bread was passed along with a plate on which was molded a mound of creamy-yellow country butter. Later, they feasted on large pieces of cinnamon-sweet apple pie, still warm from the oven, and served with slivers of cheddar cheese and mugs of fragrant coffee.

Talk at dinner was of the busy summer ahead, the many tourists who would be arriving from all over the state, and the plays Shawn was directing for the summer season.

When Nora unobtrusively began removing plates, Stacey rose quickly to help clear the table, anxious to tell her about her new run-in with Scott Lucas. Safely out of hearing of the others, Stacey confided her impulsive declaration of intention to open an antique store.

"Now, I've got to do it," she added grimly.

"But that's wonderful, Stacey! I'm really glad. I hoped you'd stay, and this seems a great way for you to do it."

"I'm not sure," Stacey said doubtfully.

Nora gave her a spontaneous hug and whispered, "Whenever I feel uncertain about a decision myself, I turn it over to the Lord. It really works. Try it."

About ten o'clock the gathering broke up, and after good-nights all around and invitations to visit and promises to call from everyone, Stacey left.

Driving home, she could not remember ever being with a nicer, more interesting group of people. Good food, fun, and fellowship were a winning combination. There was none of that sour aftertaste of other evenings she had spent in the city, where almost always someone had too much to drink, the talk was superficial, or some suggestive joke or dubious remark had marred her enjoyment. This had been a thoroughly pleasant evening. The sweetness of her new friendship with Nora gave Stacey an especially warm feeling.

She was too wide-awake when she reached the house to go right to bed. Trinket was in a frenzy of welcoming barks and dances as she came inside. She fixed herself a cup of warm milk to relax and poured some into a bowl for the little dog as well.

She tried to think of Nora's word of encouragement about the antique store project. She could not quite place it. She got out her concordance along with her Bible to help her faulty memory, sensing a slight guilt. It had been quite awhile since daily Scripture reading had been a habit. After she looked up the reference, she thumbed through the Bible to Proverbs and found the one Nora had given her.

Trust in the LORD with all your heart,
And lean not on your own
understanding;
In all your ways acknowledge Him,
And He shall direct your path.

Stacey closed the book thoughtfully. She couldn't have found better advice. Some of the confusion she had been feeling — the sudden clutches of panic whenever she thought of her rash statement to Scott Lucas — began to subside.

There was no pressure, actually. No need to make an immediate decision. Tomorrow she could take another inventory of the house and its contents, give it all more thought, time, *and prayer.* She had two months to make up her mind whether to stay in Woodfern and open a business or sell and go back to San Francisco.

She sipped her milk as the words of Scripture repeated themselves in her mind.

★ ★ ★

Stacey woke to a room full of sunshine. Impulsively she decided to take Leta Townsend up on her offer to ride one of her horses. When she phoned Pete Hansen, the ranch caretaker, he responded, "Yes, ma'am, Miz Townsend told me to expect you. Said you was experienced and suggested we give you Raven to ride. She's sweet-tempered enough but needs a firm hand since she's been let to roam free so much of the time. Keeping four horses exercised proper is a bit much for me and one other helper."

For all their wealth, the Townsend house was not particularly imposing or impressive, Stacey saw as she drove through the gates with the name on the rough-hewn arch above. The house itself was a simple, sprawling, white, woodframe farmhouse with dark shutters and a deep porch. She followed the drive around the house to where the barn, stables, and a fenced corral could be seen.

A stoop-shouldered, lean man in a cowboy hat, a plaid shirt, and dungarees, with the rolling walk of someone often astride a horse, ambled forward to meet her. He tipped the brim of his hat, ducked his head slightly, and drawled, "You're Miz Thornton, I guess. Well, come along and I'll show you the horses. I'm Pete," he said over his shoulder as

Stacey followed him into the stable.

She had brought small apples and some sugar lumps with her, and while Pete saddled up Raven, a beautiful black mare, Stacey went around feeding the four other horses, patting their velvety noses and murmuring individual greetings.

When her family had lived in Germany, she had been in a riding class taught by a martinet of an instructor who had been trained in the Prussian school of riding masters. She had just been advanced into a dressage class when her father was transferred back to the States. But Stacey had never lost her love of horses and had continued to ride whenever she had the opportunity. Leta's generous offer was almost like the fulfillment of Stacey's childhood fantasy of owning her own horse to ride any time she wanted.

Stacey was tingling with excitement when Pete led out Raven, saddled and ready for her to mount. From the mounting block she sprang into the saddle and picked up the reins. She leaned forward and stroked the long, elegant neck. The mare's ears twitched in anticipation and acknowledgement of her rider.

"I'd take the meadow road over the bridge to the woods," Pete suggested. "There's a pretty good trail all along the ridge on the hills overlooking the beach and ocean. It's a fairly easy climb, but it will get Raven used to your way of handling her and you used to her, too. There's a path down to the beach, but I don't know as how you want to try that yet." He patted Raven's side as he said, "You'll be fine, ma'am, long as you take it easy at first. Raven's got a gentle mouth but a strong will of her own."

"Have a good ride!" Pete called after her as Stacey started at a slow walk then eased Raven into a loping canter. She could feel the tug as Raven got into her stride, and Stacey knew she would have to show the horse at once that she was in command, alert to challenge.

Such a beauty she is! Stacey thought as they left the wide dirt road from the ranch and turned into a lovely stretch of alders in the sun-freckled woods. She felt the cool spring morning's wind on her face and the woodsy scent of the forest they were entering. A feeling of freedom and anticipation began to rise within her. What a glorious day, and what fun to be riding again!

Stacey felt the horse straining to have her head as they reached a clearing and she needed all the strength in her wrists and hands to keep the mare under control. Gradually, however, with Stacey speaking softly and steadily, holding the reins firmly, Raven moved into a gliding canter, and Stacey felt an exultant exhilaration. She and the horse were becoming one in a fantastic merging of mutual enjoyment.

In and out of shadows from the giant redwoods they rode, winding up higher and higher in a steady climb. Then at length they burst through another shaded glen onto a plateau at the top of a hill. From this vantage point, after bringing Raven to a halt, Stacey looked around and saw spread before her a gorgeous expanse of ocean, beach, and rocks on one side and on the other the town of Woodfern in miniature.

It looked, Stacey thought, like a French Impressionist painting. The houses were set in neat orchards, farm, and pastureland in patchlike squares of various shades of green, while the church steeples, the hills, and treetops were touched with brush strokes of gold from the sunlight.

She let the reins go slack for a moment as she relished the scene before her. Raven munched on the tall meadow grass while Stacey simply satisfied herself with the quiet beauty surrounding her.

"How beautiful is Thy creation, O Lord, and the work of Thy Hand." The words of a half-forgotten hymn from her childhood floated mistily through Stacey's mind.

Suddenly the stillness and meditative quality of the day was broken by the sound of shouts and the thunder of hoofbeats approaching along the woodland path from which she had come. Startled, Stacey turned in her saddle, jerking Raven's head up and around just in time to see two riders on horseback come crashing through the rush in a headlong race.

A man and a woman emerged almost neck-in-neck, and as they dashed past, the man threw a sidelong glance at her. It was Scott Lucas!

He must have recognized her, too, for although the young woman rider galloped on, he wheeled his horse sharply and cantered back, coming to an abrupt halt alongside Stacey.

"How do you happen to be riding Raven?" he demanded, frowning.

Flushing, Stacey drew herself haughtily up in the saddle and retorted, "Not that it is any of your business, but Leta gave me permission to —"

Scott gave her no chance to finish. His frown deepened. "Raven's no mount for an inexperienced rider," he said bruskly.

A flash of anger zinged through Stacey. "What makes you think I'm an amateur, Mr.

Lucas?" she asked indignantly. "How can you judge? You've never seen me ride!"

Still frowning, Scott's appraising glance checked over her riding outfit, the well-fitting, tan, English tweed jacket, the fawn twill jodphurs, and the polished boots. Then he said, "No, but someone used to riding bridle paths in city parks with tame, trained, rented horses is no match for a pasture-bred ranch horse. Raven's been known to be skittish. Leta should have warned Pete to be careful what mount he gave you if she was going to be foolish enough to grant you permission to ride. But she's inclined to act impulsively and to make foolishly generous offers."

"And you, Mr. Lucas, seem inclined to make quick judgments of situations and people!" Stacey interrupted.

"Just be careful. You don't know these woods or trails . . . or the horse you're riding," he snapped, and with that parting shot he turned his horse and started back along the trail just as his companion appeared at its opening.

"For heaven's sake, Scott!" the woman said petulantly.

"Coming!" he said gruffly, cantering to meet her.

The woman was young — a vivid brunette, with high color, delicate features, and dark wind-blown hair curling beguilingly around her heart-shaped face. She gave Stacey a long, interested stare.

As they disappeared into the woods, Stacey felt her irritation drain away along with the keen pleasure she had been experiencing before Scott's sudden unexpected arrival. Why was it that every encounter with him caused her to lose her composure?

Stacey let out her breath in an indignant sigh. How could a man be both infuriating and maddeningly attractive? Even in her irritation, Stacey had not failed to notice Scott Lucas's "young Lochinvar" looks, the sun gilding his hair to a tawny gold. He'd had on a russet, fringed, Western-style shirt and a wide-brimmed hat and rode his chestnut horse with the dash and confidence of a rodeo star. Stacey had to admit she had strange, mixed feelings about this man who kept intruding into her new life.

Raven twitched her ears nervously, shook her head, and tugged at the reins, as if sensing Stacey's uncertainty. Stacey leaned over to pat her soothingly and said, "It's all right, old girl. We're O.K. I know what I'm doing. We're getting to know each other, right? No matter what Scott Lucas thinks or says."

She rode back to the Townsends and returned Raven to the waiting Pete for a rubdown and bucket of oats.

"It was great!" she assured Pete when he asked her about her ride. But as she headed toward her car to drive home, she was forced to confess the meeting with the enigmatic Scott Lucas had taken away some of the pleasure of her morning and left a disturbing emotional residue.

Stacey had promised Nora to attend her church the next Sunday morning. She had hesitated to accept the invitation, but Nora had rushed to say, "I really wish you would, Stacey. Our minister is special, and I think you'll be surprised."

Stacey was finding it hard to refuse Nora anything. She had already been so friendly, helpful, and supportive. But as Stacey dressed to go, debating about the proper attire for Woodfern church-going, she heard the bells of all three churches in town echoing through the clear spring air.

At the sign "WOODFERN COMMUNITY CHURCH" Stacey turned into the parking lot. About the same time, she saw the familiar Phillips van come to a stop there. If they had not seen her immediately as they got out, Stacey might have turned right around and driven home. She was not at all sure she wanted to be stared at as a newcomer and stranger at the service.

Nora waved, smiled, and called that she was taking Brendan to the nursery and to wait right there so they could go in together. Jeff, hair slicked down and dressed in a tan corduroy jacket and freshly pressed khakis, shyly approached and walked with Stacey toward the entrance. "I hear you're thinking of going into business here," he said.

"Well, that's about all so far, just thinking."

"Take your time. Don't rush into anything and get in over your head. Nora's crazy for you to stay here, but there are a lot of hidden toe-trippers in starting a business."

Still waters run deep, thought Stacey. *Jeff's quiet but smart.*

Nora joined them and they mounted the wooden steps and went inside the church. To her own astonishment, once she was inside the tastefully painted blue-and-white interior and seated in the worn, golden oak pew alongside Nora, Stacey began to relax. She had received a few curious looks, but all of them were followed by warm smiles and nods to Nora and Jeff that included her.

She admired the beautiful stained glass window over the altar depicting the Good Shepherd. Four others on each side of the church. Looking at the one nearest her on the left she read the dedication on the brass plaque underneath it: IN LOVING MEMORY OF

ROLLIN LUCAS, 1898–1918. Picking up the hymnal in the rack in front of her, she opened it only to see another confirmation of what Nora had told her. Printed on the bottom of the title page was the inscription "Donated to Woodfern Community Church by the Lucas Family." The Lucas name seemed to permeate every facet of life in this area.

The sound of the organ made her turn in that direction and to her surprise she saw Fay seated there playing the first chords of one of the hymns. A rustling noise and a friendly pat on her shoulder alerted her to the arrival of Neil and Aris in the pew behind them. Stacey felt the same comfort of being surrounded by friends as she had the other evening.

The minister took his place, and the congregation stood for the opening hymn, then were seated to hear a short but very insightful sermon. Its scriptural base seemed particularly significant, as the minister spoke about seeking God's guidance in all things. At its close there was expectant hush throughout the church, then Fay played the overture to one of Stacey's long-time favorite hymns.

A rich, tenor voice filled the church with the song's beginning words: "O Lord, my God, when I in awesome wonder consider all the worlds Thy hands have made. . . ."

Stacey felt her scalp prickle as the notes

rang through the small church. The fullness of the voice rose unwaveringly, causing her to respond with emotion to the meaning and splendor with which the words were sung. Instinctively she looked at Nora, who dropped one eyelid solemnly in a sly wink. Stacey willed herself not to turn to see who was singing, but somehow she knew without doing so.

"Would you ever have guessed it?" whispered Nora, squeezing her arm as they came out into the noon sunshine.

"No, I would never have expected Scott Lucas to be a church soloist. Frankly, I guess I would never have thought he'd be in church," she added with a guilty grimace.

Nora laughed her delightful laugh, then led Stacey over to a small group of her friends with whom Jeff was already talking. After being introduced, Stacey let the talk swirl around her. She was facing the church doors and unconsciously watched the slow-moving exit of the congregation. Then she saw Scott come out, stand for a moment at the top of the steps, and scan the crowd before his glance caught hers.

Their eyes met and held for a second. He gave her a stiff little nod; then staring straight ahead, he walked briskly down the steps and across the churchyard. In spite of herself, Stacey's eyes followed him. He was walking toward his sports car when a yellow convertible, its top down, rolled up in front of the parking lot. It was driven by the same pretty, dark-haired woman Stacey recognized as his riding companion of the other day.

She called his name and waved. Scott paused, then gave her an answering wave and started toward her.

"Looks like Trish Findlay's back in town," said someone beside Stacey. The name meant nothing to Stacey then, but it would come to mean a great deal to her very soon.

Chapter Six

"You did know Scott Lucas was on the city council, didn't you?" Nora asked Stacey as they sat at the kitchen table in the Valentine house.

Stacey looked blankly back at her friend, then slowly shook her head. "No, I didn't. But that just about does it, I guess. What other obstacles could I come up against in getting this business off the ground?"

She felt tired and depressed. The whole past week had been spent getting through the endless red tape of obtaining permits and licenses needed for starting the Carousel.

Absent-mindedly Stacey took a second spoonful of sugar and stirred it into her coffee, then guiltily remembered reading that sugar caused just such feelings. She pushed the sugar bowl away from her, frowning. If only it were that simple to solve her other problems, ones that had nothing to do with sugar, like Scott Lucas.

"I thought once I got my business license I'd be all set. But that only seemed to start all the other problems. First, I found out that Crescent Beach Road isn't zoned for commercial enterprises and that I would have to get a waiver to the city ordinance in order to establish a business out here, and that means going before the city council. Now, you tell me Scott Lucas, who has done everything he could to buy my property, is one of the members I've got to appeal to in order to open my antique store!" Stacey put her head into her hands in mock despair and groaned.

Nora giggled. "Oh, come on, Stacey. It won't be that bad. We'll get all our friends to attend the meeting Tuesday night, and we'll be there supporting you. After all, he's only one member of the council. There are five, you know. And three of them we know very well." She patted Stacey's shoulder comfortingly.

"You make it sound like a piece of cake!" Stacey accused her. "You're not the one who's going to have to stand up there and make a pitch."

"Speaking of cake, have another cinnamon bun." Nora handed her the basket in which she had brought the freshly baked rolls to Stacey that morning. "It's going to be fine, Stacey. Don't worry."

In spite of Nora's cheerful encouragement,

Stacey was uneasy about appearing before the city council. For the entire week after she had been put on the agenda for the following week's meeting, she wished a hundred times she had never gone ahead with the idea.

And yet, everything seemed to confirm her decision. She had been in Woodfern nearly six weeks. She had come to love the little town, the climate, and especially the people. The Phillipses had drawn her into a circle of wonderfully warm, interesting, intelligent people. All of them had thought the store a solid idea that had every chance of success. Nora even confided that her prayer group had prayed about the wisdom of the enterprise, and all felt they had received a positive response.

Stacey had kept repeating all these things to herself, bolstering her own confidence, and calming the butterflies in her stomach all day Tuesday.

The city council meeting began at seven-thirty, and Stacey's appeal was about midway through the night's agenda. But she planned to be there for the beginning of the meeting, for she hoped to gain some courage by watching other people make their requests.

Getting dressed, she changed her outfit twice. She wanted to strike just the right note in her appearance, not too "citified," yet capable of running a business.

Finally deciding on a royal blue, textured wool dress with a mandarin collar, flared skirt, and set in waist, she accessorized it with a silver monogram pin and small silver hoop earrings. Then she stepped back to study the effect in the full-length mirror. Well, it might not wow them, but at least it was becoming, and that shade of blue always made her feel confident. Confidence was surely something she needed this night.

Stacey had grabbed her short wool jacket, her purse, and her car keys and started for the front door when its bell was rung sharply. She ran to answer it to find Nora on the porch.

"Just wanted to come by before the meeting and give you a little gift," she said with a smile.

"Oh, Nora!" exclaimed Stacey as Nora handed her a small cardboard box. As she took it something inside jangled.

"What in the world?" She shook it again and heard a merry tinkling sound.

"Open it and see," suggested Nora.

Juggling her purse under one arm, Stacey got the top off and brought out a small cluster of metal bells.

"For the door of the shop," explained Nora, beaming. "Every store has to have a bell to let you know when a customer comes in!"

"Oh, Nora, you are an optimist. You're really sure there's going to be a store and customers, aren't you?"

"Of course."

"Thank you for your prayers and your encouragement and . . . just for being you! What would I do without you?" Stacey demanded sincerely.

"We'd better get going. It's nearly time. We'll see you there!" she said and ran down the porch steps and out to the van, giving Stacey one final "good luck" wave.

Stacey entered the meeting room of city hall and took a seat near the front. The room was already partially full, and buzzed with murmured conversation. She could feel curious eyes boring into her back, and she tried to busy herself by reading the printed agenda she had picked up from a stack on the table at the entrance. Her breathing began to slow down somewhat, and she felt sure that somewhere in the room Nora must be sending encouraging prayers toward her. She started to turn around and see if she could spot Nora and Jeff in the crowd but just then someone else caught her attention.

Scott Lucas had come in from a side door near the platform with five chairs and a long table behind which the council members sat. He was in conversation with another man but he looked over in her direction. Their eyes met, without warmth, across the room.

Stacey felt an agitated little flutter and quickly dropped her glance to the agenda as if studying it carefully. As she did she saw her name: Thornton, Eustacia V.; Application for Business License. *Well, here we go!* she thought as the gavel was pounded and a gravelly voiced man announced loudly, "Woodfern City Council meeting is now called to order."

Stacey watched Scott Lucas mount the steps to the stage and take his seat. He moved with ease and assurance, as confident among the ranchers, farmers, dairymen, and small-town folks as he probably was in posh homes in the city. Tonight, dressed in his plaid shirt, jeans, and cowboy boots, was he playing a role?

Stacey knew from Nora that he had attended the best prep school in California, been on African safaris and Swiss ski slopes, and been entertained by millionaires in South America. She could not help being curious about this puzzling man who did not fit neatly into any specific category.

The business of the evening moved slowly. If she had not been so anxious about her own petition, Stacey would have been bored by all the parliamentary procedure they seemed to feel necessary to the process of the meeting.

When her own request for a waiver of zoning came up, there was a sharp exchange among the council members. The discussion was led by Scott.

"I see no pressing reason to waive this zoning at this time. Crescent Beach Road has always been zoned residential, and I vote against allowing a business enterprise in a section of the county that is largely agricultural." He cleared his throat and continued. "Besides, we have an antique store here in town."

"But that's mostly restoration hardware, Scott. Miss Thornton plans to deal with quality furniture, china, crystal, and valuable pieces," Tom Redwick interjected. Tom was a carpenter friend of the Phillipses and had been out to discuss with Stacey some of the possible work needed on the house. She knew he was enthusiastic about the idea of the store and had seen and admired some of the things.

The debate continued for some five or ten minutes; then the mayor called for a vote. Stacey held her breath. There were three ayes and two nays, one other member voting with Scott.

A ripple of applause and murmurs of approval moved throughout the meeting room as the mayor announced, "Petition to open a store for the purpose of selling antiques granted to Miss Eustacia Thornton."

The meeting was adjourned shortly afterwards, and Stacey found herself surrounded by the Phillipses, Shawn, Val, Aris and Neil, and other friends congratulating her.

"I think we should celebrate!" Nora said, clapping her hands excitedly. "Why don't we all go over to the Ice Cream Emporium and —"

"Ruin my diet?" moaned Aris.

"Just this once won't hurt," urged Fay who weighed a mere ninety pounds. "Come on, it'll be fun."

"Why is fun always fattening?" Aris asked, putting on a pitiful expression.

"I'll be along in a few minutes. I just want to check something out with the council clerk," Stacey said as everyone started to leave.

Two of the council members coming down from the platform stopped to shake her hand and congratulate her.

"I think you'll be a real asset to Woodfern," Clay Moore told her, pumping her hand heartily.

As she stood thanking them, Scott Lucas stalked by without glancing at her. Stacey felt lightheaded with the release of tension and victory. She had done it even with the powerful Scott Lucas's opposition. But now that she'd won she felt a little scared.

After getting her answer from the clerk, Stacey walked out of the now empty meeting hall into the lobby. She had started toward the outer door when she heard her name called and turned to see a tall figure slouched against the wall near the entrance. His outfit was that of a cowboy, and except for a huge silver belt buckle initialed LVR he was dressed in black. He did, indeed, look like all the villains of all the Westerns she had ever seen. The thought amused her at first, until she saw the look on his face as he advanced toward her with a slow, deliberate walk.

"My name's King Steele." He spoke without removing the cigarette that dangled from the corner of his hard mouth. His eyes were narrow slits in a sharp-featured, leathery face, so set it was impossible to read any clue to what he might be thinking. There was no doubt as to his meaning, however, when he started talking.

"You and your kind are troublemakers out to change things around here. Well, let me put you on notice Woodfern's been doin' fine all these years without a bunch of city people and hippies tellin' us what we kin do and not do. You may have thought you won tonight but don't celebrate too soon. Mebbe there's some of us that don't like the idea of a lot of tourists cluttering up our town and our roads."

Stacey stared at him, momentarily immobilized. Again she had the feeling of watching something in a movie melodrama or on TV.

At that King Steele turned his back and strode out of the building. Stacey felt a cold shiver course down her spine. There had been no mistaking the hostility in the man's eyes and something of an implied threat in his words. King Steele was mean. He was the kind who would stop at nothing to implement his prejudices. And obviously she was included in his hostile contempt for "outsiders" and "hippies."

For a moment she felt very vulnerable. Then she remembered Nora and her friends waiting at the ice cream parlor, and the many others who had come up to her after the meeting to say, "Welcome to the business community of Woodfern."

Determinedly Stacey tried to shake the aftermath of uneasiness from the unpleasant incident. But as she went outside and found her car, she had the eerie feeling that somewhere in the shadows she was being watched.

Even the light-hearted laughter and gaiety of the gathering at the Ice Cream Emporium did not erase the disturbing undercurrent lingering from the encounter. Nor did it help any when Stacey asked Jeff quietly if he knew anyone named King Steele and received the unsettling answer: "Sure. He's the foreman at the Lucas Ranch."

Remembering the open hostility in the man's eyes, Stacey had to suppress a shudder.

The unpleasant incident with Steele faded into the background during the next busy weeks as Stacey readied the house to open her store the first week in July. Nora was an enormous help to Stacey in unpacking, sorting, deciding which of the antiques to display for sale first. They spent hours in the attic in this seemingly endless task.

One day while thus occupied Nora suddenly declared, "You know, it's just occurred to me while we've been doing this . . . I mean, I've never seen so many cut-glass bowls, sterling serving pieces, and whole tea sets of china. I think they must have been wedding presents! Some of them are barely unpacked, never used. Or maybe they were for a hope chest. Girls used to have them in the old days. Even before they were engaged, they often started very young to collect beautiful things for their future homes." She held up one delicate crystal goblet to the light slanting in from one of the dormer windows, and her voice trailed off wonderingly. Then she met

Stacey's eyes. "What do you think?"

"I believe maybe you're right," Stacey agreed slowly.

"Miss Valentine never married, did she?" asked Nora.

Stacey shook her head. "Actually she's sort of a mystery to me. Our family lived overseas for so many years Mom lost contact. Aunt Eustacia was the youngest in my grandmother's family and took care of their elderly parents until they died, then lived here alone."

"I wonder if she had planned to be married and something happened. These things were never unpacked. . . ."

"I really didn't know much about them at all. When I found the house and property had been left to me, I was totally surprised."

"It seems a bit sad, doesn't it?" Nora said softly. "I mean, if she had planned to be married and use all these lovely things herself."

"I believe you must be a misty-eyed romantic, Nora," Stacey teased.

"Well, yes, I guess I am. Isn't every woman?"

Stacey shrugged and went on unpacking as she said, "I might have been when I was younger; I'm not so sure now. I grew up believing Doris Day movies. You know, where she and Rock Hudson, no matter what the complications or the misunderstandings, ended up starry-eyed and singing into the sunset? I used to watch them on TV when my dad was stationed in Germany and Japan. They didn't get many first-run American movies, just the oldies and —" she paused, laughing, "you haven't seen anything until you see Doris Day being dubbed in Japanese! Anyway, those movies were harmless enough in themselves — not like today's R- and X-rated ones — but I'm not sure about the effects being all that harmless. I mean, I grew up with a lot of unrealistic ideas about romance, about love, about relationships gleaned from just that sort of 'harmless' movie." She stopped unpacking for a minute and looked at Nora directly. "What I want to know is whether that kind of romantic love's fantasy, or is it possible?"

Nora returned Stacey's confrontational look.

"No, it isn't possible, Stacey, not unless God's at the center," she said simply. "That's the important element of any relationship. After that a man and woman can create a good marriage."

Just then their conversation was interrupted by a voice calling to Stacey from the bottom of the attic stairway.

"That's Paul," she said scrambling up from her knees and going to the head of the steps. Paul Chambers, a carpenter, contractor, and friend of the Phillipses, had been going over the house for Stacey to see if it met all the requirements of the building code for a commercial establishment. He and his wife, Jan, were completing the restoration of a Victorian house at the edge of town which they planned to make into a bed and breakfast establishment.

"Everything checks out O.K., Stacey. But I think you're going to need new wiring throughout pretty soon. These old houses can be firetraps if you get a short or a faulty circuit." Paul pushed back his duckbilled cap and grinned up at her. "This place is a real beauty. I've been under the house, and the studs are solid redwood. They don't build houses like this anymore," he said admiringly.

"Thanks so much, Paul, for all you've done. And remember what I said. When you and Jan are ready to furnish your B and B, I want you to come out and select a bedroom set."

"I'll hold you to that!" Paul gave her a salute. "Well, I'll be on my way now."

Stacey had learned that among the friends she had made through the Phillipses that bartering was a way of life.

After Nora left, Stacey found a box containing some exquisite lace curtains, yellowed with age, but in otherwise perfect condition. With careful washing, bleaching, and ironing, they would be just the right touch for the bay windows in the two front parlors.

She was just trundling down the stairs with the bulky carton when she saw a car turn into the driveway, and a few minutes later Larry Meade was coming up the porch steps. Stacey opened the door to his jaunty salutation. "So you did it! Good for you!" he declared. "I wasn't sure the great Lucas juggernaut wouldn't annihilate you!"

Stacey just smiled and invited him in. "Come and have a look around. It's not quite ready to open yet, but you can get a pretty good idea of how it will look in a few days."

The two front rooms downstairs opening on to the hall were for display and arranged to resemble a family parlor and dining room of the 1880s. Graceful settees, armchairs, and marble-topped tables were placed in conversational groups; Staffordshire spaniels were set on the mantelpiece below a floral still life in an ornate frame on the wall. The other room looked ready for a formal Victorian dinner party, the table set with gold-edged china, cut-glass bowls, and crystal goblets.

"Fantastic!" Larry commented enthusiastically. "You've done a phenomenal job. It should be a huge success."

"Thank you. But I had lots of help. Would you like some coffee? I was just ready to take a break myself." Stacey led the way toward the kitchen. As Larry followed her through the hallway he stopped to admire a walnut roll-top desk. His hand slid appreciatively over the smooth wood and he said, "Say, this is exactly what I've been looking for. I'm planning to do over my office. A country lawyer has to have a roll-top desk!" he said, grinning. "How much?"

"I'll have to check in my dealer's hand-book," Stacey answered. "I'm new at this, you know. I'm still learning."

"Whatever it is, put a 'sold' sign on it. That'll look good to your first customers, any-way. I won't have it delivered until I finish painting the interior," Larry said.

After sharing a cup of coffee, Stacey walked with Larry out onto the front porch. As they stood chatting about her plans for the garden, Scott Lucas's yellow jeep went by. As he passed he turned his head briefly, then just as quickly turned away and drove on staring straight ahead.

"It must really gall him to drive by here every day on his way back and forth to the ranch, knowing he couldn't get his hands on these six acres," Larry commented dryly.

"I keep wondering why these six acres were so important," Stacey remarked. "From what I hear the Lucas Ranch has plenty of land."

"But the Valentine property joins the Lucas spread at this end, and that's what he wanted. . . . I don't know why, except Scott Lucas has a lust for land."

Stacey looked startled, then shocked. "That's a terrible thing to say about someone — anyone!"

"Why, if it's true?" Larry demanded. "The Lucas family has always wielded power around here. Maybe it's in the genes. They're used to getting what they want. Although —" Larry paused and became thoughtful. "Scott wasn't always like that. He was a nice kid growing up. But then a lot of tragic things happened in a short time. Scott's mother died, then Dan, his older brother, was killed in Vietnam, and six months later, his father, Bryan Lucas, crashed his private plane into a mountain coming back from Montana. That's when Scott came back here, took over the ranch, and began to run it. Whatever ambitions he might have had he had to give up. There was no one left, and the Lucas holdings were tremendous."

"What kind of ambitions?" Stacey asked. In spite of her antipathy toward Scott Lucas, she found him an interesting if enigmatic person. His image did not mesh with the man whose voice had thrilled her in church that morning.

Larry shrugged. "I'm not sure. Scott was

93

different when he came back. Serious, with-drawn, kept his own company and counsel. Doesn't socialize much. At least, not with those of us he grew up with around here." Larry shook his head. Then, as if finished with the subject, he smiled at Stacey and said, "Well, I'd better be off. Congratulations again, and good luck on your opening." With a wave he went down the steps and out to his car and backed out of the driveway.

At last everything was in readiness for the Carousel's grand opening. The lace curtains were starched and hung, the furniture gleam-ing, the floors polished, and outside on the porch, the hanging baskets of fuchsia and trailing lobelia swung gaily.

In town to place her opening announce-ment ad in the *Courier*, Stacey purchased a new mailbox to replace the rusted one at the end of the driveway. Afterward, she ran into Leta Townsend at the post office.

"Glad now you took my advice, young lady?" she asked Stacey with mischievously twinkling eyes.

"I'll know better a week from now, I guess," Stacey replied, laughing.

"I'm glad I met you. It'll save me a call. I want to invite you to the picnic we always have on the Fourth. We have a wonderful fireworks display. Fred's a real kid about the

Fourth and fireworks. You will come, won't you?"

"Thanks, I'd love that!"

"Good. See you then. And, of course, I'll be coming by the day you open the Carousel," Leta promised as she headed out the post office door.

Preoccupied with sorting through her mail as she left the post office, Stacey nearly collided with someone coming in. An apology sprang to her lips until she found herself looking into the steely eyed face of King Steele. For a moment their eyes locked; then Stacey murmured something and hurried past, a chill feeling causing a little shudder. Just outside, across the street, she saw the pickup truck with the distinctive Lucas Valley Ranch logo painted on its side, and behind the wheel was Scott Lucas. He did not see her, and Stacey turned in the other direction to her parked car. One encounter with someone from the Lucas Ranch was quite enough for one day, she decided.

Chapter Seven

On the morning of July 2, Stacey walked through the downstairs rooms with a sense of delight and accomplishment. For the first time in weeks there was nothing to do.

She decided she would drive down to Nora's to give her a thank-you gift for all her help. Stacey had scrubbed and shined to a lovely glow a copper teakettle which Nora had admired when they were unpacking boxes. Today was a good time to give it to her as a surprise.

Stacey showered and put on fresh jeans, noting with some satisfaction that all the jeans she now owned were beginning to have that bleached-out look and the soft, comfortable feel of long wear. They were about all she wore these days, and she loved it. It was a far cry from the way she had "dressed for success" every day as a career woman.

As she paused at the end of the driveway to turn into the beach road, Stacey gazed proudly at the carousel horse restored and mounted under the hand-lettered wooden sign ANTIQUES. She was now in business!

Even though it had only been a few months, her life in San Francisco had faded far into the background of her full, busy life in Woodfern. Already she seemed a different person with new goals, changed ambitions, an altered perspective. Much of her change was due to Nora and the people she had met through her. It was as if her whole life had been turned around and set in a new direction.

Stacey was amazed how quickly her old restlessness had disappeared. Life here in Woodfern was distilled to a simplicity that Stacey found appealing and satisfying. Little by little she had become convinced that moving here and opening the store was God's plan for her. She had found a purpose, friends, and a new faith. She was even thinking in Scripture! She'd got that from Nora, she thought amused.

What a wonderful friend she had found in Nora and how pleased she would be with the kettle, Stacey thought. Nora was as interested and intrigued at the treasures they had found in Aunt Eustacia's attic as she herself was. It was Nora who had first come to the conclusion that they might have been unopened wedding presents.

She felt a little sad thinking of the unfulfilled hopes and dreams the unused wedding presents symbolized, the garden gazebo built — perhaps for a wedding that never took place.

"I'm getting sentimental!" Stacey warned herself. "Poetic, romantic . . . maybe weird?"

She had never thought of herself as a sentimentalist, crying at sad movies or romance novels, or weeping at weddings. Except once. When her parents had repeated their marriage vows at a special ceremony at their thirtieth anniversary, Stacey had found her eyes misting so much that the candle flames and flowers on the church altar had blurred.

That they would want to do that after so many years of marriage made Stacey realize how special the relationship was between her mother and father. It was the kind of marriage she hoped one day she might have. But she was no longer sure it was possible. Stacey still remembered the timeless beauty of the traditional wedding vows. Did people still believe in the "forever" of those promises? Jeff and Nora seemed terribly in love. She would have to ask Nora about their wedding.

"Oh, it was perfect!" Nora exclaimed, eyes shining at Stacey's question. "We were married in a little country church and the reception afterward was in the pastor's own garden.

We were both new Christians then, and everything had a special glow."

Nora had just baked bread, and the small kitchen was filled with its fragrance. She took a loaf and sliced the heel off it, pushing forward a round of butter stamped with clover impressions. "Help yourself," she told Stacey. "There's beach plum jam, too."

Stacey pulled the rocker she was sitting in closer to the table and Nora's tiger-striped cat jumped into her lap. She stroked it absentmindedly as she spoke. "It's nice to hear about two people finding each other and having that kind of love. I got so tired of the game-playing connected with dating in the city. I began to doubt if the 'real thing' really existed. Was there a man out there somewhere who wanted —" Stacey broke off feeling rather embarrassed for having almost put into words her longtime dream.

"A man who is your 'Mr. Right'?" Nora finished for her.

Stacey flushed and nodded. "I guess, something like that."

"It's not only finding the right person," Nora continued softly. "It's being the right person, the kind of person *your* right person can love!" She laughed her rippling, light laugh. "That sounds sort of convoluted, doesn't it? I just mean if I'd met Jeff a few years before I did . . . I wouldn't have been the right person for him. I was sort of mixed up for a while. My folks got divorced when I was thirteen and I was pretty angry and rebellious. I went through a lot. But Jeff did, too, in his way, even though he'd been raised in a Christian home. But, the Lord's timing is always right. We met at the right time for both of us."

Stacey left Nora's about an hour later feeling good about herself and the world in general. She always felt that way when she had spent time with Nora. "Thank you, Lord, for giving me Nora for a friend!" she whispered as she went down the winding, rutted hill road.

Reaching the bottom, Stacey swung left impulsively, instead of turning right to go back toward town. She knew the Lucas Ranch was on a bluff overlooking the ocean at the end of the country road, and she was curious to see it.

White board fences marked the beginning of Lucas land, and then she passed a high T-shaped gate with the familiar logo over it. She pulled to the side of the road and saw a rambling, white clapboard and fieldstone ranch house, with barns, stables, corrals branching out around it. It looked exactly as a ranch should and like one Scott Lucas would run.

Satisfied, yet strangely irritated, Stacey

started her engine and drove on to the end of the road where the beach and ocean were spread out in a panoramic scene before her. She got out of the car and walked along the water's edge for a good half hour. Happiness swelled within her, and she knew with certainty that this was where God had placed her and all that she had done was part of His plan for her life.

She got back in her car and started up the road again. As she was passing the Lucas pasture, she suddenly braked, not really believing what she saw. The car sputtered, then stalled and came to a stop, and Stacey coasted to the side of the road to get a better view of the field. She blinked. It couldn't be! Llamas? It wasn't possible!

The scene in front of her was something straight out of the pages of the *National Geographic*. Llamas belonged in South America not northern California — didn't they?

But she knew she was not mistaken. The strange, furry, oddly gaited animals grazing peacefully in Scott Lucas's pastures were undoubtedly llamas.

Chapter Eight

Getting ready to go to the Fourth of July party, Stacey felt excited. It was fun getting dressed up for a change. She had worn nothing but jeans for weeks. She chose a sleeveless blue linen and took along a darker blue cardigan because in Woodfern even midsummer evenings turned cool.

There were already several cars parked in the Townsends' curved driveway when she arrived and as she went up to the house she could hear the sound of voices and laughter coming from the patio. Leta answered the door herself and escorted Stacey through the house out to the sheltered terrace.

"I think you know most everyone here," she said, taking Stacey by the arm, "and those you don't you soon will! Everybody just mingles and gets acquainted at our parties. There's Neil and Aris over there talking to Val, and of course you know Shawn. Nora's here somewhere with the children. You know how they all adore Nora. We won't have the fireworks until it's really dark. In the meantime, eat and enjoy, won't you? I've got to keep Fred busy barbecuing hamburgers for the kids or he'll start the fireworks early." She chuckled and shook her head. "He's such a kid himself."

Stacey joined Fay at the buffet table which was appropriately decorated for the occasion in red, white, and blue.

The food was sumptuous and varied. Besides the tantalizing hamburgers Fred was grilling at the barbecue, there were sliced ham and turkey, several kinds of salads, various breads and rolls, and corn-on-the-cob and baked potatoes kept hot in large aluminum pans over electric burners. On another table were assorted soft drinks in big tubs of ice, pitchers of iced tea, and a coffee urn.

Stacey was hardly seated at one of the redwood picnic tables when something made her look up just in time to see Scott Lucas arrive. On his arm was one of the most attractive young women Stacey had seen since coming to Woodfern. Her short, dark hair framed a gamin face, and luscious red lips outlined perfect white teeth in a dazzling smile.

"Here comes the debutante!" murmured Fay.

Stacey studied the daughter of one of Lucas Valley's oldest, wealthiest ranching families.

Trish Findlay certainly had the look of a thoroughbred with the proud set of her head, the beautifully proportioned body in a kelly green silk blouse and tailored white slacks.

Obviously, she was the product of a privileged childhood, of early vitamins, the best orthodontists, ballet lessons, gymnastics, horseback riding, and the best schools. Recently she had had the advantage of expert advice from color consultants and hair stylists, plus good designer clothes.

Trish Findlay appeared to be as rumored, the girl who had everything, and from the way she kept him in proprietary tow, she had Scott Lucas as well. Just as Stacey drew that conclusion she caught Nora's mischievous look of understanding and blushed.

To the west the sky was almost totally dark, and a ripple of anticipation circulated especially among the children as Fred began to set up for his famous display of fireworks.

Stacey saw that Scott and Trish had found places at one of the picnic tables opposite hers, and she was conscious of avoiding looking at them. She told herself it was inevitable and reasonable that they should be together. After all, they were both from pioneer families in the area, both heirs to vast land holdings, property that if merged would make a magnificent combined heritage. Both were young, healthy, handsome, and probably expected to carry on the tradition their ranching forebears had passed on to them. They were, as the saying went, "made for each other."

But why, then, were Stacey's thoughts mixed with odd feelings of irritation and annoyance? An unwanted feeling of loneliness began to steal up on her as she looked around and saw that, besides herself, all the other guests were in couples.

"Time for the fireworks!" announced Fred and Stacey's pondering on the possible relationship between Scott and Trish Findlay was interrupted.

The first sound of a rocket whooshed through the air, and a second later sparkling splatters of color burst into the dark sky accompanied by the ooohs and aaahhs from children and grown-ups alike. They watched the most spectacular private fireworks show Stacey had ever seen. It was a glorious, exciting, colorful display, and Fred Townsend was having as good a time putting it on as were all the wonder-struck children and admiring adults. The finale, a shimmering American flag, was wildly applauded and then, two by two, people started to leave. A few of them came over to Stacey to say goodnight and wish her well on her grand opening the following Saturday. They promised to come by the store that day.

As she thanked them, Stacey became aware that Scott was standing a few feet away, alone for the moment. He looked as though he were waiting until she finished her conversation with Shawn and Val — as though he wanted to say something. She turned toward him, and he seemed about to speak, but at that moment Leta touched her arm and she turned back. When she looked again, Trish had rejoined Scott and was laughing up at him gaily.

It might have been Stacey's imagination, but Trish's glance, as she pulled Scott playfully along toward the gate, seemed somewhat like a cat who had just lapped up a saucer of cream meant for someone else. It smacked of being triumphant.

And that smacks of being 'catty'! Stacey rebuked herself as she was driving home. Still she couldn't help wondering what Scott had been about to say to her.

That was only one of the unanswered questions in her mind about Scott Lucas. After her conversation with Larry Meade, Stacey found herself even more intrigued by this enigmatic man. In this sheep and cattle ranching country, why was he raising llamas?

She was almost ready to turn into her driveway when her headlights shone ahead on a dismaying sight. Her brand new mailbox had been overturned, and the stump of the post was splintered as if by an ax blow.

Stacey jammed on the brakes, and leaving the headlights on high beam she jumped out of the car and ran over to examine the damage.

The shiny metal box was dented, and part of her new address, "The Carousel, Antiques, E. Thornton, Crescent Beach Road" had been scratched off. The post would have to be replaced.

How had it happened? Had a car run off the road and hit it? Had joy-riding teenagers swerved into it, knocked it over? Or had it been vandals?

Troubled, Stacey got back in the car and drove past the fallen mailbox into the driveway. She let herself into the dark, empty house. She could hear Trinket's wild, welcoming bark and frantic scratching from the back porch where she had been left. As Stacey hurried to let the little dog out, she wondered if Trinket had heard the commotion undoubtedly caused by the overturning of the mailbox.

After her first night here, Stacey had never been afraid of being alone in the house — even though Trinket had an unnerving habit of pricking up her ears and growling, then sometimes dashing to the front door to bark. Although it was probably a chipmunk, squirrel, or some other harmless creature on a nocturnal foraging expedition, Stacey was reminded uncomfortably of another night she had been convinced there was a prowler.

The experience had faded until tonight. Stacey had been so occupied, so happily involved in her plans for the Carousel, that she had forgotten lying sleepless the rest of that night and fighting fear.

Attempting to reassure herself, Stacey reminded herself that small communities were always riddled with rumors, gossip, and suspicion. It might be that the Valentine family, and she as the present owner, were the brunt of some old hostility, unsolved problem, or grudge, and someone was taking it out on her, working off resentments by senseless hassling or malicious pranks.

She went into the kitchen, turning on lights as she went. She got out a saucepan to heat some milk. A cup of warm milk to insure a sound night's sleep and to chase away any lingering uneasiness was just what she needed.

But in spite of sipping it slowly and reading a particularly complicated catalogue of antiques to dull her into drowsiness, Stacey lay sleepless for a long time. This night's happening confirmed her suspicion that Scott Lucas was not the only person in Woodfern who had not welcomed her coming nor wanted her to stay and prosper.

Chapter Nine

The days of summer passed like those sequences in films of the pages of a calendar flying off to mark the rapid pace of time. From opening day through the early weeks of September, Stacey's business thrived beyond her best projections.

"It only goes to prove that God does 'exceedingly abundantly above all that we ask or think'!" Nora said, her eyes twinkling, when an awestruck Stacey named the sum of one month's earnings.

Stacey had made a kind of pact with herself, a mental reservation, that she would give the store a trial run to see if it could provide her with an income at least equal to her salary at the gallery in San Francisco. She had already extended the sublease on her city apartment to the present tenant. That had been a frightening step for Stacey. It meant she was going to stay in Woodfern and make a go of her business.

Besides the constant flow of tourists — both shoppers and browsers — the other businesses in Woodfern had generously supported Stacey, sending her customers and referring collectors to the Carousel.

On the day she had opened, the Woodfern Florist truck had made several deliveries to bring her plants with congratulatory cards from the Chamber of Commerce and other shop owners. It seemed that only one person begrudged her occupancy of the Valentine house and establishing a business. *Make that two,* Stacey thought, adding a mental postscript as she remembered Scott's scowling foreman, King Steele.

But there was so much friendliness, so much genuine warmth from most of the people with whom she came in contact that little by little the initial reception she had received from Scott and his ranch foreman receded to the back of her mind.

There had been one reminder of her own unexplainable reaction to Scott the night of the Townsends' Fourth of July picnic supper. One day during the second week after the shop opened, the house was filled with milling customers asking questions about items and prices. Stacey had been at her busiest when out of the corner of her eye she had seen Trish Findlay enter the display room.

She did not seem to be looking for anything in particular. She just walked about, stopping here and there to pick up a small ceramic dish or crystal piece, then put it down. She moved closer and closer to where Stacey was talking with a customer, and Stacey had the distinct feeling she was being watched closely. Under most circumstances she would have been nervously self-conscious. But the antique she was discussing had an especially interesting history, and Stacey became engrossed in conversation with her customer who was quite knowledgeable about eighteenth-century furniture.

When she had looked around again, Trish was gone.

Had she really come to buy something or just to take a good look at the "new girl in town"? Had Scott told her about their stand-offs? The idea of Scott discussing her with Trish Findlay made Stacey squirm.

Stacey stayed too busy most days to dwell on these unanswerable questions and fell into bed each night both exhilarated and exhausted. She found she had much studying and catching up on antiques to do, for she was learning that many of her customers were experts in the subject. In order to do a better job of selling, Stacey usually took a book to bed to read until sleep overcame her.

One Sunday, late in August, she was invited to brunch after church at Aris and Neil's. The invitation gave Stacey's conscience a guilty nudge. Since that first Sunday when she had gone at Nora's invitation, Stacey had not returned on her own. She had meant to go, but once she opened the Carousel, there always seemed to be something waiting for her attention on Sunday morning.

In spite of her guilty feelings, however, Stacey felt a lift of anticipation as she drove to the picturesque, white, wood-frame church. It reminded her again of the ones she had seen in almost every small New England town. She really loved going to church, even though she had gotten out of the habit after the first year she lived in the city. Now she determined she would attend regularly. After all, she had so much to thank God for in her new life.

Inside she spotted Nora's red-gold hair from the shining halo made by the sun slanting through one of the stained-glass windows. Stacey slipped into the end of the same pew, and Nora gave her a delighted smile as she passed her a copy of that Sunday's bulletin.

Unconsciously Stacey's eyes moved down the page to see if the title of the soloist's hymn was given, and she knew in that moment, that part of her eagerness to come to church was caused by the chance of hearing Scott's fine,

113

rich voice and experiencing again her surprising emotional response to it.

But no special selection appeared on the schedule of the day's service. Stacey felt a twinge of disappointment, then gave herself a mental shake. Why in the world did her thoughts so often turn to that infuriatingly enigmatic man — a man who consistently kept his distance and gave every indication that the less contact he had with her, the better?

And yet, it was this very thing that intrigued her. Everything she knew about him now seemed contradictory. His background and outward image conflicted with that of a man who chose to sing spiritual songs in a little country church on Sundays. And what a voice he had! A voice like his did not spring full-blown into being. It was a trained voice, not one that strained or reached for notes, but flowed in velvety perfection.

What had Larry Meade said about Scott? Something about after his brother and father died, he'd had to give up "whatever ambitions he might have had and come back here to run the ranch." Had those ambitions had anything to do with his marvelous voice?

Stacey impatiently pulled her wandering thoughts back to the Scripture verse given as the basis for Reverend Thomas's sermon. But as the junior choir filed in and the congregation rose, Stacey glanced up to the illuminated window of the Good Shepherd behind the altar and suddenly the lambs that surrounded Him seemed to become llamas!

Stacey blinked, swallowed, and sternly focused her attention on the minister as he mounted the pulpit. These random thoughts of Scott Lucas had to stop invading her mind she told herself crossly.

Later, as they were seated under the trellised arbor of the Brady's sun-shaded patio, relishing crisp buttery waffles with homemade blackberry syrup, Stacey, with managed casualness, asked Nora, "Where was the famous soloist this morning?"

Aris who overheard answered, "Scott Lucas? On a stock-buying trip out of the county, I understand."

"Maybe out of the country even!" Neil interjected. "He's been in the store buying books on South America."

"Your place is a regular mecca of local news," declared Shawn. "I wonder why the *Courier* doesn't annex it to their composing room. If you want to find out what's happening in Woodfern, just go in Neil's bookstore. I guarantee you'll find out everything you wanted to know but were afraid to ask!"

The general laughter that followed this remark covered Stacey's embarrassment at having seemed to be interested in Scott Lucas's whereabouts.

Business at the Carousel slowed nearly to a halt by the end of September with only a few late season vacationers stopping in to look and make an occasional purchase.

"Business really drops off for a while now, until around Thanksgiving," Neil Brady told Stacey. "But in December, just wait!"

Nora had already informed Stacey about December in Woodfern. "It's absolute magic!" she explained excitedly. "Shawn actually started it, then everyone caught the spirit and it just grew and grew. When they started the Little Theater the first year, they put on Dickens' *A Christmas Carol*, and it was a huge success. The next year they did it again, and since then it's become a tradition. But what's developed from it is amazing. For three weeks before Christmas, the whole town is turned into a bit of "merrye olde England." Main Street is decorated, almost every store has its own Christmas tree, and at night the lights are fantastic. Most of the shops stay open later in the evenings, and the clerks all dress in old-fashioned costumes of the 1800s. It's like a party all the time."

"That sounds wonderful! I've been to the Dickens Faire in San Francisco a couple of times, but it only lasts one day. They have

116

vendors roasting chestnuts, puppet shows, mimes, and all sorts of festivities," Stacey said.

"Well, just imagine what three weeks is like! It's so much fun. The Lamplighter Restaurant stays open late so people can go there for dessert after the performances. And, of course, the waitresses and waiters are all in appropriate costumes, too. People come from all over to attend the play, shop for Christmas presents, eat, and enjoy themselves. It's a real family sort of thing to do."

In the meantime, between the dwindling crowds of September and the promise of December, there were days when nobody came to the Carousel at all.

"It doesn't really matter," she confessed to Nora. "I've already made more this summer than I dreamed I would. Now, I have the funds for the new wiring Paul suggested, and I can have the outside of the house painted in the spring. I love the way he and Jan painted their Bed and Breakfast Inn with all the gingerbread trim in a bright color contrasting with the siding."

Late one evening in October Stacey was repairing the cane seat in a wooden chair she had rescued from the collection in the barn when the phone rang. As soon as she answered it, she heard the incredulous voice of her friend Kim in San Francisco.

"You can't actually mean you've decided to stay in that forsaken spot and live there! You're a city girl, Stacey. The novelty of that place is bound to wear off soon, and you'll come tearing back!"

Stacey laughed. "Don't be too sure. Believe me, I love it here!"

"Okay, come on, spill it. There has to be a reason." Kim paused, then said, "I *know* there's a man. You've met someone super!"

"Don't I wish!" Stacey gave a fake moan.

"That *has* to be it!" persisted Kim. "You can't be happy living in an old mansion in an isolated corner of northern California selling antique furniture. That's not you." Another significant pause: "There has to be a man behind all this — *somewhere!*"

Stacey toyed for a moment with the idea of telling Kim about Scott Lucas, but then decided against it.

"I'm sorry I can't convince you," she finally said.

Frustrated, Kim changed the subject. "Well, when are you coming to the city? You can stay with me since you've been foolish enough to give up that great apartment."

"Probably not until after Christmas. People tell me after the Christmas rush I'll need a vacation."

"Is that a promise?" asked Kim. "I miss you. I have no one to confide in, no one to let down my hair to . . ."

Stacey laughed. "Yes, it's a promise. I'll let you know when I'm coming."

After they hung up, Stacey suddenly realized how different her friends in Woodfern were from the ones in the city. Kim was sharp — smart, sophisticated, up on the newest trends and the latest styles — whatever was in. Yet at heart she was a wonderful person. Stacey wondered how Kim would fit in here. More to the point, how would *she* fit in now with her friends in the city? She had changed a great deal in many ways — some obvious and some subtle. Life was simple since she had come here. She was beginning to put down roots like the bulbs she had planted in the cleared flower beds of the old garden. How they would grow and bloom, though, she would just have to wait and see.

Indian summer lingered late. With fewer customers in the shop, Stacey went riding more. Although Raven remained her favorite of the Townsends' horses, she rode others after Pete told her none of them got enough exercise.

Stacey looked forward to those hours spent in the saddle. She became more familiar with the trails and most enjoyed the ones through the redwoods on the cliffs above the beach. As she became more confident, she rode longer and farther and farther from the Townsend property, exploring new and different paths through the surrounding woods.

She often packed a light lunch and then stopped at some vista point to tether her mount, letting the animal graze while she ate her sandwich and gazed down at the waves crashing against the rugged rocks below. It was a never-ending panorama of beauty. These quiet interludes became times of spontaneous prayer and meditation for Stacey. She was discovering new spiritual depths in herself and always came back to the house renewed and refreshed.

Toward the end of October, Stacey began waking to light frost in the mornings, and there was a definite snap in the air when she took Trinket out for a brisk walk. Some nights now she put an extra blanket on the bed and considered sleeping downstairs on the old sofa in the big kitchen as she had the first night she arrived instead of in the drafty upstairs bedroom.

One Wednesday afternoon in the first week in November, Stacey found herself half-heartedly rearranging a glassware display in a large, curved, bevelled-glass china cabinet. There had been no customers all morning. In fact, there had been none all week. Motivated by her own restlessness, Stacey hung a "CLOSED" sign on the front door, got into her riding clothes, and drove over to the Townsends'.

The sky was overcast, and hovering clouds tumbled in a kind of chaotic movement above. The air felt soft, but the possibility of rain this soon in the year was remote. Pete grumbled as he brought out the saddled Raven. "My old war injury aches like crazy. Betcha we'll have rain 'fore evening. I wouldn't go too far or stay out too late today, Miss Thornton."

Inwardly amused at Pete's pulling an old saw like a weather-vane war wound, Stacey just nodded and headed Raven up the trail through the hills. There was something exciting about the rising wind which sent a rustling sound through the trees and lifted the mare's silky mane. Raven seemed to feel it too, for she shook her head impatiently, tugging at the reins until Stacey loosened them and let the mare move into a gallop.

Leaning forward, Stacey felt her own exultation as they pounded through the woods. A feeling of absolute freedom rushed through her as they went faster.

They came into a clearing at length, but instead of the light they usually encountered after riding through the dense shadows of the towering redwoods, the day seemed to have darkened rapidly. Halting at the edge of the woods and lifting her face skyward, Stacey felt the first drops of rain. They fell slowly at first, little more than a mist. Raven tossed her head, twitched her ears nervously, and blew through her nostrils, all the time stamping and shifting her feet.

Stacey wondered if she should turn and go back the way they had just come or if she should go forward to a dirt road that would eventually lead back to the Townsends' ranch.

She thought she remembered taking a less-traveled trail to the left one day and going down a well-marked path between boulders and onto the beach. Once she reached the beach, she knew she would have no trouble finding the road and making it back before she was totally drenched.

There was no time for hesitation as the rain began to come down heavily, so she wheeled Raven to the left and plunged into the forest.

Chapter Ten

In a matter of minutes Stacey felt enveloped in darkness. The ominous clouds overhead and the woods through which she was riding increased the sensation of blackness. The sound of the rain pouring down through the trees echoed the thudding of her horse's hooves.

As she hunched over Raven's neck, she realized how foolish she had been not to pack a poncho under the saddle. She had been alerted to these unpredictable winter storms — the torrential rains that began without much warning and often lasted for days. Winter on the north coast, she had been told, was stormy and fierce, but she had been lulled into forgetting by the lovely fall which had lingered through October.

Well, now she was paying for it.

Needles of icy rain pelted her mercilessly. By now her jacket and sweater were drenched, the fabric of her jodphurs clung to her thighs, and her hair was soaked and dripping into her eyes.

The ground underneath the layer of pine needles became soggy as the horse pushed along, wading through the thick underbrush as Stacey tried to find a path leading out of the woods.

With one hand she dragged the wet strands of hair back from her face, trying to see a little better through the driving rain. Finally, a long distance away she could see a faint light. Maybe there was a farmhouse nearby, she thought, and hope began to stir within her. She urged her tired horse on. "Come on, old girl. Let's find you a shelter and maybe a pail of oats up there. Let's go!" she whispered hoarsely, patting Raven's neck. She gave the reins a tug.

Gamely the horse struggled forward, and Stacey bent almost double to shield her face from the stinging onslaught of cold rain. The chilling cold pressed in on her, and her hands were numb from the leather reins cutting into them.

The light grew closer, and Stacey raised her head to see the long, low outline of a ranch house — at last. Her heart leaped with thankfulness. "Thank you, Lord!" she whispered.

Lights were shining through the yellow squares of the windows. Inside there would be warmth to dry the aching chill out of her cramped bones and there should be a barn or some sort of shelter for her tired horse. She turned Raven toward the house and urged her to go the few yards that separated them from it.

As if she knew instinctively that rest and feed were near, Raven gathered a last spurt of strength and broke into a trot. Then with a whinny and a shake of her head she came to a stop under the overhang of the deep shake-covered roof of the house.

Stacey eased her cold feet out of the stirrups, slid off the horse, and stood for a moment resting her head against the soaking mane.

"Good girl," she said hoarsely, patting Raven's nose. Then with a sigh Stacey sloughed through the mud to the front porch of the house. She was so tired her legs dragged with each step. Exhausted and shaking, she leaned against the heavy oak door and hammered on it with a numbed fist. The sound of approaching footsteps accompanied by loud barking came from behind the door.

"Quiet, fellow," a man's voice ordered.

Then the door was flung open so suddenly that Stacey nearly fell into the arms of the tall man standing there. She lifted her head, pushing back her wet, tangled hair and gasped.

"You!"

Scott Lucas' mouth twisted in a wry smile. "I could say the same thing, Miss Thornton. I didn't exactly expect to see you at my door on such a night and in such a condition."

A kind of helpless fury swept over Stacey. Of all the people she needed to ask for help, why did it have to be Scott Lucas? But the situation was too desperate to let her pride deter her.

"My horse, Raven . . ." she said in a strangled voice. "We got caught in the storm . . . I got lost. . . ." She took a deep breath. "She needs —"

"Come in," Scott said crisply. "I'll get one of my men to take care of the horse right away. You need to get out of those wet clothes and warm yourself." He held the door open wider and Stacey stumbled in. She felt the whip of the dog's tail against her legs, and his wet nose pressed into her hand. He began a kind of low whimpering as if to say he understood her predicament. Irrelevantly Stacey wondered if this were the same dog who had challenged Trinket that day in the parking lot. But she was too tired to know or care.

Scott had left the room to give directions about Raven, and Stacey stood in the archway of the wide hall looking into a large living room where a fire crackled in a massive stone fireplace. Walking stiffly she went over to the hearth and held out her chilled hands to the heat.

Behind her she heard the sound of Scott's boots on the bare, polished floor of the hall, and a minute later the sound of men's voices, then the sound of a door slamming.

Stacey turned around, her back to the fire and glanced about curiously. So this was where Scott Lucas lived. She wondered if the man reflected his environment, or if it projected his strong personality.

Her instant impression was of relaxed, masculine comfort. The firelight cast a russet sheen on the redwood-paneled walls. Floor-to-ceiling bookshelves stood on either side of the fireplace, and two leather sofas faced each other across a burled redwood coffee table. On one wall was a collection of native Indian baskets and on the other a handsome gun case. Instead of the deer heads or antlers she might have expected to see mounted around the walls, there were several large oil paintings, one a seascape, another the best Stacey had yet seen of sunlight slanting through redwoods, and another of a desert scene.

Scott came back in the room. He stood for a moment regarding her with a frown. "You'll catch a terrible chill if you don't get out of those things. You're soaked to the skin. Come back to one of the guest rooms and have a hot bath. Look in the closets. You're sure to find something you can wear while we dry out your clothes."

"But I should call . . ." Stacey stopped, feeling foolish. There was no one for her to call, no one who would be worried about her failure to come home. The Townsends' man expected her to see to Raven and put her in the barn herself as she usually did, so he would not have waited for her.

Scott interrupted whatever she was going to say. "No way to call anyone. Telephone lines are down from the storm. The radio reports the river is reaching flood stage, so the bridge will be closed to vehicles by now."

Scott shook his head but looked amused as he said, "I'm afraid, Miss Thornton, you'll have to spend the night here as my guest." He was observing her reaction as he went on. "Unfortunately, there's nothing you or I can do about the situation. So we'll just have to try to tolerate each other and make the best of it. Come, I'll show you the way."

There was no alternative. Stacey, already feeling the combined effects of exhaustion and chill, followed him to the end of a wide hall where Scott opened a door.

She stepped into a bedroom surprisingly luxurious for a ranch house, or for her idea of what a ranch bedroom should be. A handsome, polished-brass bed with a satin quilted spread sat against the far wall. To the right, twin amber-velvet Victorian chairs and frosted glass lamps accented the deep piled, gold carpet.

"The bathroom is adjoining, and I think you'll find everything you need. When you're finished, come back to the living room and we'll have something warm to drink." He paused for a moment, looking at her enigmatically. "I suggest we hold back our hostilities and call a truce for tonight, due to the impossible circumstances. Don't you agree?"

Without waiting for an answer, Scott went out, closing the door quietly.

The bathroom was sumptuous. A raised, bronze-tiled tub was surrounded by gold shag carpeting. Thick-piled brown and gold towels were stacked on glass shelves beside it, and on its edge was a huge abalone shell filled with scented soaps.

Within minutes Stacey was soaking in warm fragrance, her aching muscles gradually easing. It was like a dream, she thought, closing her eyes after her harrowing ordeal.

After a long while, she roused herself from the warm water, wrapped herself in one of the velvety towels, then padded out to the bedroom and slid open the doors of the wide closet.

Quite an assortment of women's robes, all different styles, hung there. Stacey was not surprised because Scott had told her to take her pick. But she could not help wondering how often Scott "entertained" women at his secluded ranch. A handsome, wealthy bachelor and a world traveler must have many women friends only too willing to spend time with him here. Or maybe it was *de rigueur* among the wealthy to provide leisure wear for unexpected overnight guests.

She selected a turquoise, velour caftan with a cowl neck and wide, flowing sleeves. It was zippered to the hem. Then she brushed her damp hair until it was dry. She had lost the scarf she had been wearing to tie back her hair in the storm, so she had to let the blond mass hang loose. In one of the bureau drawers she found some slipper-socks and pulled them on. She was standing uncertainly, wondering what she should do next when a tap came at the door followed by Scott's voice saying, "Whenever you're ready we can have dinner."

She took a few steps across the room to the door; then her hand froze on the doorknob. For a moment her bizarre circumstance overwhelmed her. Marooned by a torrential storm at an isolated ranch, she was cut off from the world for who knew how long with a man who from the beginning had shown open antipathy. Stacey was momentarily suspended between wild panic and hilarity. She doubted that even Ann Landers would have a solution for this situation. Well, as he had suggested himself, all they could do was make the best of it.

To her surprise, the dog was waiting in the hallway as if to escort her back to the living room. Stacey put her hand on his large, silky head and felt the swish of his tail against her legs. Could she have been wrong about the dog? Was she wrong about his master as well?

Scott got to his feet as she came into the room. "Feeling better?" he asked casually.

"Yes, thanks," Stacey murmured, feeling suddenly shy.

"Some coffee?" he suggested, gesturing toward the tray containing a beverage server and cups. "Or maybe you'd like a brandy to take the chill out?"

Stacey shook her head. "Coffee, please."

He poured her a steaming cup. "Sugar, cream?"

"Sugar, one lump." She took the cup he handed her.

"Your horse has been taken care of, rubbed down, fed, and stabled."

"Thank you. You've been very . . . kind." Somehow the words were hard for Stacey to get out.

Scott shrugged as if it were of no consequence.

"I thought we could eat here in front of the fire. It will be warmer than the dining room tonight, and you should probably stay warm after the drenching you got," Scott said briskly. "I'll tell Manuel we're ready."

A smiling, dark-eyed, young man in a white jacket rolled in a serving cart. With a nod to Stacey, he quickly and efficiently laid a cloth on the coffee table, and placed on it a tureen, a covered basket, two plates, bowls, and silver.

"Hope you like clam chowder," Scott said as he seated himself on the other leather sofa opposite Stacey.

"Love it," she said, putting her spoon into the hot creamy soup and tasting it.

"French bread?" He passed her the basket containing chunks of buttered, toasted bread.

They ate silently for a few minutes. Then Stacey spoke a little hesitantly, "I do want you to know how grateful I am. If I hadn't stumbled on to your place — well, I don't know what I'd have done."

She remembered his warning about inexperienced riders on unfamiliar trails the time she had encountered him in the woods the first day she had taken Raven out, and was glad he didn't make any comment. *Give him points for that,* she added to herself.

"I would have felt terrible if anything had happened to Raven. Leta was good enough to allow me to ride her horses, and Raven's a favorite of both of us."

"Are you and Leta good friends?" Scott asked. "Did you know her before you came here?"

"Yes, to the question, are we friends. And no, I didn't know her before. But she came to the house the first morning I was here. In fact, Leta's the one who suggested I open my antique store."

Scott made no comment on that.

Manuel appeared with another tray.

"More chowder?" Scott asked Stacey.

"No thanks, it was delicious," she said as Manuel took her bowl and replaced it with a serving dish of a delicately poached filet of sole and a baked potato.

"We eat simply —" Scott said, a smile tugging at the corners of his mouth, "— when we aren't expecting guests."

Stacey felt her color rise.

"Don't be embarrassed. I was only teasing." His voice was gentle.

Surprised, she looked up and saw he was smiling.

"Look," he said. "Do you think we could pretend we'd never met before? Or better still, that our previous encounters had not been so — so abrasive? We're probably going to be stuck here together for quite awhile. I think it's time we got to know each other without all the leftovers of hostility or past mistakes."

Stacey's eyes widened with surprise, and her lips parted in a smile. "Yes, I'd like that."

"Tell me about yourself," he began.

Outside the storm raged. The wind wailed around the corners of the house battering the windows with pelting bursts of rain. But inside, the firelight glowed cheerfully, and as they talked, Stacey forgot the weather.

Scott had spent a year between high-school graduation and college traveling through Europe with his roommate. They had hiked in Switzerland, ridden motor bikes through France, and backpacked through the Austrian Alps. Since Stacey had spent much of her life in some of the same places, they had fun recalling those they both enjoyed.

Time passed almost unnoticed. Manuel had taken away the dinner things, brought fresh coffee, and left again.

A log broke and fell apart, and Scott stood up to attend the fire, adding two more logs and stirring it into a crackling flame. He replaced the poker, drew the screen, then turned to Stacey. "Would you like to hear some music? I warn you I've got fairly old-fashioned taste — show tunes, musicals." He laughed a little sheepishly.

"That sounds fine," Stacey replied. She curled up in a corner of the sofa, tucking her feet under her. Scott went over to the bookcase that housed his stereo and tapes.

Soon the familiar, lilting melody of the overture from *Camelot* began to fill the room. Stacey couldn't help smiling. It had always been one of her very favorite plays, and she loved the music.

Scott came back to the fireplace and stood looking into the fire, one arm leaning on the mantelpiece. His expression relaxed as he listened. Stacey saw it devoid of the anger, annoyance, or any of the other negative emotions she had so often seen registered on it. It was a fine, strong face, a face with character, she thought.

As if conscious of her gaze, he turned and smiled at her, and inexplicably Stacey felt her heart skip a beat.

A sudden, sharp sensation seized Stacey, stunning her with its implication. She dared not believe the thought that had come into her mind. *It doesn't happen like this,* she told herself. Yet, something within her assured her that something, indeed, was happening — something that might change her life.

Scott knocked his pipe ashes against the

brick and said slowly, "You know, I had a completely different impression of you. I thought you were a career-minded, assertive, take-charge, city woman. . . . Funny, how first impressions can be totally wrong . . ."

Stacey laughed softly, "I was thinking exactly the same thing about you."

Scott grinned, looking suddenly boyish. "I guess we both got off on the wrong foot. I take the blame . . . entirely. I came on so strong and was out of line. It was just that I was so sure . . . I mean, I'd been told —"

"Sir! Excuse me for interrupting." Manuel's apologetic voice came from the doorway where he stood looking anxious.

Scott turned. "That's all right, Manuel. What is it?"

"May I see you for a moment, sir?"

"Of course, excuse me," Scott said to Stacey and followed Manuel out of the room.

The music of *Camelot* was still playing, and Stacey hummed along with the tenor's voice singing those poignant lyrics, "If ever I should leave you, it wouldn't be in summer . . ." She closed her eyes. This had to be the most romantic love song ever written.

"Come here!" Scott's voice called from the doorway. He was grinning and he beckoned her. "Hurry! I want to show you something."

She unfolded herself from the sofa and

walked quickly to where he was waiting. He took her hand and led her through the hallway to the back of the house and into the kitchen.

The ranch kitchen was modern and streamlined with white enamel cabinets, stainless steel counters, an island with a wide, wooden chopping block set into more work areas on both sides, and every conceivable cooking appliance and gadget.

On entering, Stacey was puzzled. Did Scott want her to admire his kitchen? Then he tugged the hand he was still holding and said, "Look!"

She looked in the direction he pointed and saw in the corner a plump woman in a big rocker, holding in her arms something creamy and fluffy with erect cocoa-colored ears and Bambi-like eyes wrapped in a baby blanket. The lady was feeding it with a large nursing bottle.

It was too big to be a lamb. What in the world was it? Stacey wondered; then it dawned on her. It was a baby llama!

"He's one of our 'preemies,' " Scott explained. "And Gloria is our 'llama mama,' " he chuckled. "She's Manuel's wife. They're both from South America. I brought them back with me on my last trip so Manuel could go to school in the States. Meanwhile he works for me here on the ranch. As you saw tonight, he's a great cook. And Gloria! Well, she's one of the seven wonders of the world. Gloria, meet Miss Stacey Thornton."

Gloria, whose huge dark eyes sparkled, smiled and nodded. Manuel explained, "Gloria's still learning English. She's a little shy about speaking yet."

Stacey moved cautiously closer, bent over and tentatively touched the stiff, velvety ears. "How adorable!" she breathed.

"Would you like to trade places with Gloria for a while?" asked Scott, behind her.

"Could I?"

"Sure."

In two minutes the transfer took place, and Stacey found herself seated in the deep rocker, the bundle on her lap. The llama had not missed a beat, but went right on sucking, although the big, brown eyes with incredible lashes had taken in the change.

"They like to be held securely," Scott told her.

With the warm weight nestled against her, Stacey rested her elbow on the arm of the rocker and shifted the bottle slightly into a more comfortable position and looked down at the silly little face. It was as cunning and irresistible as it could be — like something out of an animated Disney feature. She smiled delightedly up at Scott.

He hunched down beside the rocker — the look on his face tender and open. Their eyes met over the llama's fuzzy head, and Stacey almost drew in her breath audibly. It was a moment of such intimacy — more than if they had touched. She was the one who had to lower her eyes.

The only sound in the kitchen was the nuzzling noise of the baby animal's mouth gulping the formula from the nipple.

"I've just started experimenting with raising llamas in this climate and altitude. We're exploding a lot of myths about them. They're a lot hardier and more adaptable than anyone thought they would be," Scott said after they had returned the drowsy baby to Gloria and watched her tuck it into a special, blanket-lined box.

The Labrador, who had been sleeping with his head between his paws in front of the fireplace most of the evening, looked up and stretched as they entered the living room. Scott leaned over to stroke the dog's head and was rewarded by two or three thumps of his tail.

The music from *Camelot* was still playing. Now it was at the place in the movie where Richard Burton, as King Arthur, was giving that last, poignant description of his dream to the boy. They listened until the finale crescendoed and the sound went off. Scott went over to take the tape out. He shook his head slightly and said, "Sometimes I wonder if I'm not a little like poor Arthur myself. Trying to create something entirely new with my llamas where no one has ever done anything around here but raise dairy cows, beef cattle, and sheep. Maybe it will all come tumbling down around me like Camelot."

"Don't say that!" Stacey said sharply. "I mean, it's wonderful to have a dream, to do something entirely new . . ." she broke off. She realized she was describing her own efforts at the antique store.

But Scott apparently didn't make that connection. He came back and sat down on the couch opposite her again.

"That's what I feel and think, too. Of course, I wouldn't replace the stock my father is known for producing on this ranch. His reputation was too good for me ever to change. But that part of the ranch practically runs itself. My foreman was here in my father's time, and most of the men have worked for the Lucas Valley Ranch most of their lives. I couldn't and wouldn't want to do any other kind of ranching. But —" he gestured enthusiastically with both hands, "it's important to me to do something creative . . . something that hasn't been done around here before. I'm going up to visit a successful llama ranch in Oregon soon. I've been to South America twice and learned everything I could there. If I decide to go into this in a bigger way, I'll have to go down there again to buy some breeding stock . . ." He broke off. "I'm probably boring you."

"No, not at all," Stacey said.

But Scott stood up. "Well, I've said enough. You've had a very long, tiring day. I suggest we call it a night. Would you like a nightcap, something to help you sleep?" he asked.

Stacey suppressed a yawn, then laughed. "I really don't think I'll need anything."

"Then, we'll say good night."

"Good night and thank you again, for everything," Stacey said and started toward the door.

"Good night, Stacey," he said, and she stopped and turned, smiling. It was the first time he had called her by her first name.

"Good night . . . Scott."

Sheer muscular exhaustion made it difficult for Stacey to go to sleep immediately in spite of the huge, luxurious bed. But the cause of her wakefulness was this crazy situation of being under the same roof with Scott Lucas — a situation she could never in her wildest imaginings have thought possible.

Nothing happens by chance. The phrase floated back to her now. "The lot is cast into the lap, but its every decision is from the Lord." *Even the events that seem accidental are really ordered by Him,* she thought drowsily.

From somewhere in the house she heard the low sound of music. Scott was playing *Camelot* again.

Chapter Eleven

Stacey woke to a raw, gray day with a fierce, chill wind. It had stopped raining, but the sky still hung heavy with threatening clouds that promised more storm to come. From the window of the guest bedroom she could see that the beach had been swept clean by the receding tide. The sea tumbled with turbulent waves.

She found her clothes, dried and pressed, hanging outside her door. When she walked into the living room, a fire roared in the stone hearth and a tray with coffee urn and cups had been set on the low table in front of it.

She poured herself a steaming cup and was relishing its invigorating warmth when a voice behind her spoke. "Good morning! Sleep well?"

She turned to see Scott standing in the archway. As he came forward she was aware of the clean, outdoorsy scent of him mixed with a fresh, herbal fragrance that must be his shaving lotion. He wore a rust wool shirt over a ribbed, tan turtleneck and biscuit brown cords.

"The radio weather report says there's another storm front headed our way. And the bridge to Woodfern is still under water." He poured himself a cup of coffee, then gave Stacey a half-rueful smile. "So it looks as if you'll have to extend your stay at Lucas Ranch."

"I'm a bit worried about my little dog," she said, the concern evident in her voice. "I have one of those automatic feeders and she'll have plenty of water. It's just —"

"Well, maybe one of your friends has gone by to check on you," he suggested. "Anyway, we can probably get you home before the new storm breaks."

"You don't think I could ride Raven back?"

He looked dubious. "I don't think it would be a good idea. Certainly not the way you came. She seemed a little lame when I checked her this morning. Oh, don't be alarmed. It's nothing serious. She's just somewhat stiff. Probably strained a leg muscle. Another day's rest and she'll be fine, I'm sure. Anyway, we can put her in the horse trailer and take her back to Townsends' in my truck. So don't worry."

"I hate to impose on you this way."

"Hey, do I look imposed on?" he demanded, smiling. "I suggest we make the most of our day even if we are marooned."

He rubbed his hands together, held them out to the fire.

"I've been up since five, and I'm ready for something to eat. How does a real, ranch-style breakfast sound to you?"

Programmed by her childhood as part of a service family whose unwritten law was instant acceptance and adjustment to any circumstance, Stacey fell in with Scott's obvious good humor.

A real, ranch-style breakfast as served at the Lucas Ranch was far different from the one glibly advertised on most restaurant menus, Stacey discovered. Seated at the dining room table and surveying the array of food Manuel placed before her, Stacey thought of her usual morning fare of cold cereal and juice. There were steak, mounds of creamy scrambled eggs, hash-browned potatoes with onions, feathery light baking powder biscuits, pancakes, and maple syrup.

"Do you eat this kind of breakfast every morning?" Stacey finally asked Scott.

Helping himself to a second serving of eggs, Scott shot her a surprised look, then grinned and answered in a put-on Western drawl. "Why, shore. This here's a workin' ranch, ma'am. We hands need a passel of energy to do our chores."

"I believe it!" she said, laughing at his performance. More amazing than the size of the breakfast, Stacey mused, was the easy, comfortable camaraderie she and Scott seemed to have fallen into.

When they got up from the table, the day outside had darkened considerably, and they stood for a few minutes in the graceful bowed window to view the changed scene outside. Beyond the sea wall at the edge of the front sweep of lawn, a gale-force wind was lashing the ocean into a mass of rolling waves that flung themselves against the rocks. It was near noon, but the sky looked like dusk.

"The storm seems to have come sooner than expected," Scott commented. "Do you play backgammon?"

"No."

"Come on, I'll teach you," he offered.

The afternoon, which could have been boring or uncomfortably strained, turned out to be fun and interesting. Stacey caught on quickly when Scott explained the game, and they spent an hour or more at the challenging play.

A curtain of fog had dropped suddenly while they were occupied, and they did not notice it until Manuel brought in their lunch to have in front of the blazing fire. The gray sheet of fog had cut off the sight of the sea, and when Manuel drew the drapes, the room became a warm enclosure of comforting intimacy.

"This has been an amazing set of circumstances," Scott remarked as he cut and served Stacey a generous slice of mushroom quiche. "Under what other possible conditions would the two of us ever have got past our unfortunate beginning and found we are not only compatible but that we actually like each other?" He smiled at her, his blue eyes twinkling. "You know that old question, who would you like best to be stranded on a desert island with? Well, if I'm ever asked who I'd like to be trapped in a northwest Pacific storm with . . ."

"That is, of course, if you've packed our backgammon board," Stacey added.

"Of course. Incidentally, you're very quick. And intelligent, and attractive, and —"

"Oh, please!" she held up both hands.

"O.K., but seriously. Would you have ever believed we'd find each other so . . . congenial?"

"Maybe it's what they call 'lifeboat psychology.' You know, you find yourself in some sort of desperate situation with a group of people you've never seen before, and suddenly . . . bingo! Everyone is bonded, everything works."

"Possibly," conceded Scott.

Stacey steered the conversation to another subject by asking, "I know you sing — I heard you one Sunday at the church — but do you also play the piano? I saw the baby grand in the alcove in the hall across from the dining room."

A shadow seemed to cross Scott's face at the question. "That was my mother's piano. She played beautifully. In fact, she was studying at the Conservatory when she left to marry my father. But she continued studying and playing just for herself and the family. Yes, I do play a little to accompany myself sometimes. It's just a hobby, though." He dismissed it and asked, "More quiche?"

They finished lunch, and Stacey felt she should give him a little space. She, too, needed some time away from what she was beginning to perceive as an unsettling enjoyment of Scott's company. She went to the guest room, selected a book from several in the bookcase and settled down to read and alternately gaze out at the stormy afternoon.

The fog reminded her of a musical her parents had taken her to see in London on her fourteenth birthday, a revival of a popular show of the fifties called *Brigadoon*. The story had been about a mythical Scottish village that only appeared out of the fog once every hundred years. The villagers had to make the most of that one day. Stacey remembered particularly a special song from the play because her parents had given her the album and she had listened to it often. It had been sung by the older sister of the bride of that day, who wondered if she, too, would one day be a bride. It was called "Waitin' for ma dearie," and the last haunting line was "Maybe there's a someone who's waitin' for *his* dearie . . . *me!*"

The most improbable thing that had surfaced in Stacey's mind in this whole improbable happenstance was that in this time she had spent alone with Scott Lucas, he seemed exactly the kind of man she could fall in love with — "the dearie" she had been "waitin' for" all her life. The thought stunned, frightened, and thrilled her.

How could it be? Their initial meetings had been so hostile, and even now she hardly knew him. And yet, she could not deny her heart's knowing. In many ways, he reminded her of her father. He had that same self-confidence, a certain tautness that spoke of self-discipline and control, and underneath a considerateness and a subtle sense of humor.

Physically he was very different from Colonel Thornton, but he had some of the same qualities Stacey had always admired in her father, and had unconsciously hoped to find in a man she might someday want to marry.

She almost gasped at the direction her thoughts were running. Marry! Marriage was the farthest thing from her mind. Or at least so she had thought. Certainly Scott Lucas did not have marriage in mind or, at thirty or thereabouts, he certainly wouldn't be living alone on this large, isolated ranch. Of course, he had everything — looks, intelligence, money. Still, an occasional look in his eyes made her wonder; a look of discontent, or was it unhappiness?

Her random thoughts were interrupted by a knock at the door. Stacey sat up with a start. The unread book slipped from her hands and fell onto the carpet as she got up and went to the door.

It was Gloria, the plump "llama mama," with smiling, black olive eyes. "Mr. Scott want to know if seven o'clock for dinner O.K.?"

"Fine," Stacey nodded vigorously.

It was now after five. She would have time to bathe before then. Stacey wished she had something really glamorous to put on for dining that evening, but even as the thought popped into her head she squashed it. Who was she trying to impress? It just seemed rather inappropriate to wear the checked blouse, sweater, and jodhpurs she had worn the afternoon she had started out so unwittingly on her horseback ride.

Well, come on! Stacey admonished herself. *Your daydreams about Scott Lucas are getting ahead of the reality! Don't get any ideas about him,* she warned herself as she got into the warm, bubbly fragrance of the tub. He was simply exhibiting his well-ingrained good manners by being a gracious host. In that, as in everything else, it seemed, Scott was a talented perfectionist.

There was, however, a noticeable change in the atmosphere between them at dinner. Scott was courteous but quiet. The teasing manner of earlier in the day had disappeared. They ate silently for the most part, interrupted only as Manuel removed their soup plates and replaced them with the main course, parmesan chicken, rice pilaf, and snow peas.

"We'll have coffee in the living room, Manuel," Scott told him when they had finished.

The Labrador rose to greet his master as they came through the archway, and Scott rather absent-mindedly stroked his head and then walked over to where the coffee service had been set on the burled table.

He poured their coffee, adding the one lump of sugar to Stacey's without asking, and handed her the delicate cup and saucer.

"Time's been telescoped in the last twenty-four hours," he said as he seated himself on the leather sofa opposite her and stretched out his long legs. He turned his direct blue gaze upon her. "I feel as if I've known you a long time and yet there's so much more I'd like to know about you."

She stirred her coffee, looking down into her cup, for some reason not wanting to meet his eyes.

"I thought I'd told you quite a bit about myself — my childhood with the Air Force's 'traveling circus,' " she laughed a little self-consciously, "my hit and miss education, my just managing to graduate from college, and then the incredible luck of landing an interesting job in the most fascinating city . . ."

"Those are all window dressings, actually. There are other things. For a young girl — excuse me, young woman — to pull up stakes, even shallow ones, and come to a rather remote area by herself and start a business . . . it really is unusual. That's why I —" Scott broke off mid-sentence. He leaned forward and put down his cup. "Let's play a game."

"Backgammon?"

"No. Another kind of game. I used to do a thing on my college newspaper. I was the 'inquiring reporter.' I'll ask the questions — you don't mind answering questions, do you?"

"If they're not too personal," Stacey fielded with a shy smile.

"Oh, you can refuse to answer any. But, no, they're just fun. Like — what's your favorite color? Simple questions." He smiled. "Ready?"

"O.K." Stacey said, feeling an inner tension. What if she inadvertently revealed too much?

"Give me ten of your favorite things . . . just off-hand."

"Uh-uh," Stacey looked around. "Burning logs, stormy surf, pelting rain . . ."

"Good, go on," Scott urged.

"Smell of apples, horses, lilacs . . ."

"Favorite things to do?"

"Running through wet grass in my bare feet." She giggled. "Reading the Sunday papers. Toasting marshmallows over a beach fire." She halted, her mind a blank suddenly.

"Pet peeves?" Scott coached.

"Phoniness. Cynical people. Costume jewelry. Oh, my goodness, Scott! Talking about myself!" she laughed.

"You're doing great, go on. Favorite food!"

"Don't mention food after that dinner!"

she ordered, then, "Oh, all right, anything chocolate!"

"I wish I'd made a tape of this for future reference!" he laughed.

"Now it's my turn!" declared Stacey. "Favorite things?"

"Winter storm," he repeated. "Old boots, a good book, Labradors and llamas . . . music."

"Speaking of music," Stacey said tentatively, "would you play something for me? I forgot to put on my list piano music."

Scott seemed to hesitate. Then, he stood up and said, "Well, O.K. I'm out of practice but I hate it when people say that. So let's see how it goes." He motioned her to follow him to the piano. He hesitated again slightly before he lifted the lid back from the keys and sat down. His fingers rippled through a chord, then into the familiar Debussy etude, "Claire de Lune." From that he went into a medley of recognizable refrains which Stacey could not really name. That did not stop her from enjoying his impromptu concert. She leaned on the piano just at its curve and watched with interest the shifting light and shadow on Scott's face as he played.

Almost as if it were not intentional he drifted into the music of *Camelot*, and to her delighted surprise he began to sing. From the comic "What Do The Simple Folks Do," he moved into the beautiful and touching "If Ever I Should Leave You." When he finished with a final rippling chord and suddenly stood up, abruptly closing the lid of the piano, Stacey was jolted back to reality from the dreamy cloud woven by the music.

"And that's enough of that," Scott said firmly, the bare trace of a smile softening the stern look that had come upon his face.

Feeling somehow rebuked, Stacey managed to compose her pulsating response to the music, the melody, and the man. "That was lovely. Thank you," she said in a low voice. "I think that was a beautiful way to end the evening. Good night, Scott, and thank you again."

She turned and walked quickly down the hall toward the guest room, wondering if somehow she had betrayed how deeply moved she had been.

In the safety of her room she held out both hands and saw that they were trembling. There had been one moment back there, just before he stopped singing, when it had seemed to Stacey that Scott was singing the lyrics explicitly to her. She could almost have touched the feeling in the air between them. When he had stood up and closed the piano, for one crazy moment she had thought he might just kiss her!

What disturbed her most was the way she had longed for him to do so and knew that if he had, she would have welcomed his kiss.

Chapter Twelve

Stacey prided herself on being able to sleep anywhere. But that night sleep defied her, and she tossed and turned restlessly. The new turbulence of her feelings kept her from drifting off as she normally would and the possibilities of her feelings for Scott Lucas kept her in quivering wakefulness.

"It's insane!" she told herself, pounding her pillow into a different shape and trying once more to settle herself for sleep.

She did not remember when she had finally gone to sleep, but when she awoke it was to clear skies, an ocean as smooth as blue glass, and a brilliant sun shining on a peaceful stretch of sand. It was nearly nine o'clock, she noticed by the small gold clock on the bedside table. She hurried into her clothes and went out the bedroom door. As she walked down the hall toward the front of the house she thought she heard voices. One was the clear, light voice of a young woman. When she reached the door of the living room she saw it was Trish Findlay.

"But you must have known we have our own generator at Lucas Ranch." Scott's voice was cool and even. Over Trish's shoulder he saw Stacey appear in the doorway and he lifted his chin, turning his head slightly, ready to greet her even as Trish was saying, "Well, if I ever did know, I forgot! I thought you might need —" her voice broke off, and she, too, turned in the direction Scott was looking.

As she did her pretty face instantly changed to one of shock, then petulance, then malice. Her mouth curled as she let out a long, "Well . . . it seems I've interrupted something very cozy!"

Her insinuation hung in the air for one startled moment while Stacey absorbed her full meaning. Then she felt the color rush up in her face, and an angry retort formed to repudiate the insulting remark. But before she could say anything, Scott interjected, "I don't know whether you've met Miss Stacey Thornton, Trish."

Stacey cast him a surprised look. Wasn't he going to explain her reason for being there?

"We've not been formally introduced," Trish said with a little toss of her head. "But it would appear you know her very well, Scott." Her voice was heavy with sarcasm.

Scott shrugged. "There's coffee, Stacey, if you're ready," he said nonchalantly.

All at once, Stacey was furious. Why didn't he say something that would clarify the wrong impression Trish Findlay obviously had formed. Why was he ignoring her rude behavior? Stacey was so angry at his attitude she stood with fists clenched, immobile, waiting for him to say something.

A long moment passed, tingling with tension. Then Trish, with an imperious gesture and a small stamp of her polished, booted foot, snapped, "Don't think I'm stupid or so naive I can't see what's going on here, Scott Lucas!"

With that she flounced out of the room, brushing by Stacey and down the hall to the front door. She let it slam behind her with a resounding bang.

There was another moment of silence in its aftermath. Then Stacey turned back to Scott and demanded, "Why didn't you tell her why I was here?"

"I don't owe anyone an explanation for anything I do, least of all Trish Findlay."

"But what about *me?* Didn't you even think how it looked for *me?* Didn't it occur to you that she went away from here thinking . . . goodness knows what she was thinking!" Stacey's voice rose in frustration.

"Trish was having one of her tantrums. She's had them all her life when anything hasn't suited her. No, I don't feel I have to explain your presence or any guest's presence when she barges in here on some pretext, as if we were in some kind of siege because of the storm! She knows better than that. Now, will you have some coffee?"

"No, thanks," Stacey said curtly. "If you'll have my horse brought around, I'll leave now."

Scott frowned. "You don't have to go on account of Trish. You haven't let her upset you, have you? I thought you had more sense than that."

"Can't you see the position your not saying anything has put me in?" she burst out, exasperated by his studied coolness. "You could at least have explained!"

"I've always gone by the rule of not making excuses. Your friends don't need them, and your enemies don't believe them anyway. Let Trish think what she wants. It doesn't change the truth."

"What about me, what she might say about me? I do have a reputation to protect." Stacey was getting more and more frustrated at Scott's failure to understand her anger.

"You're really being ridiculous —" he began.

Stacey cut in coldly, "Will you please have

Raven brought around, or should I go saddle her up myself?"

"No, of course not. I'll see that it's done, since you insist. There's no reason for you to be so upset. If you'd stay —"

"I've stayed long enough. *Too* long!" she flung at him, and turned on her heel and practically ran back to the guest room to get her jacket.

The brisk, cool freshness of the rain-washed morning cleared Stacey's mind of the angry confusion she had felt after Trish's enraged departure. By the time she had left Raven at Townsends' and driven home, her indignation had simmered down somewhat. She was still furious that Scott had not come to her defense against Trish's implied accusations. Even if it were against his own code of not making excuses for his actions, at least he might have considered her.

Trinket was ecstatic to see her and leaped about her with whimpers of happiness. Stacey cuddled the little dog and tried to reassure her that she was not going to leave her alone soon again. But for the rest of the day, Trinket was her anxious shadow.

In the afternoon Nora stopped by. Stacey gave her a brief version of her odyssey, and Nora was appropriately sympathetic.

"I was worried when we came by here during the storm and I didn't see your car. Everyone's electricity was off for awhile, so not seeing any lights didn't bother me. But with the car gone I thought maybe you'd had some kind of family emergency. I didn't dream Trinket was here by herself."

"There was no way I could let anyone know. The telephone lines were down, too."

"I know." Nora nodded. "Wasn't it a coincidence that you should end up at the Lucas Ranch of all places?" she commented, shaking her head in wonder.

The phrase "divine coincidence" flashed immediately through Stacey's mind and she rejected it. But after Nora left, the oft-held thought kept thrusting itself back. From childhood she had heard over and over that nothing happened by chance.

Stacey did not want to think about those magic moments she had experienced with Scott — the laughter, the quiet companionable hours in the firelight, listening to his music, and hearing him sing . . . to her! He had seemed to be looking at her as if she were the only person in the world!

It was all her imagination, she told herself briskly. It meant nothing. Certainly not to him. If it had, wouldn't he have jumped to her defense when Trish Findlay made those snide remarks?

But as much as she tried, Scott and those hours they had spent together, adrift as it were on an island surrounded by the storm, lingered hauntingly. As in *Brigadoon*, it had come like a wisp and just as quickly floated away.

Stacey busied herself with dusting, rearranging the crystal in the large china cabinet, and clearing the yard of debris from the storm. She did everything possible to keep from thinking about Scott Lucas.

She was still working in the front parlor when purple shadows of the autumn afternoon cast rectangles of rainbow-colored light through the stained-glass window onto the polished floor. The golden afternoon was quickly dissolving into dusk. Stacey shivered as she went about closing shutters, drawing curtains, and finally going to lock the front door. For some strange reason, she dreaded the coming of night and being alone in this big, old house. Just as she slipped the lock fast, the beam of headlights arced into the driveway and she stood still, watching. Who could be coming at this time of day?

Within a few minutes she knew. The tall figure striding confidently up to the porch had a definitely familiar outline. It was Scott. Instinctively Stacey tensed. What could he possibly want?

Automatically she switched on the porch light and opened the door. His expression was serious, his eyes riveted upon her. Then very solemnly he drew from behind his back one perfect rose, long stemmed and dewy fresh, its velvety red surrounded with a spray of fragile, white baby's breath and tied with a narrow crimson ribbon. He held it out to her.

"A peace offering," he said. "I thought of trying to find an olive branch or a dove —" A shadow of a smile hovered around his mouth.

In spite of herself, Stacey laughed.

"You idiot!" She held the door open wider. "Come in."

He stepped inside. She took the rose he offered. Its scent was strong, yet sweet and exciting, like the sudden pounding of Stacey's heart.

"You do accept my apology, then. For this morning . . ." Scott's words were stiff and awkward and Stacey knew how hard they were for him to say.

"Let me find something to put this in," Stacey said, and Scott followed her into the parlor where she selected a lovely bud vase from among the beautiful assortment of cut glass. Scott wandered around the room while she went to the pantry sink and filled it with water, then gently placed the rose into it. She came back holding it and found Scott standing by the old rosewood spinet. He had lifted the keyboard lid and let his fingers idly play a scale. Then he turned his head and looked up at her as the last note died away. The room was very still, and the distance between where he was and where Stacey stood, poised as if holding her breath, seemed to close about them, drawing them together.

"Pride!" Scott said contemptuously. "The seventh deadly sin! Obstinate, stupid pride! There's no excuse." He scowled fiercely. "I've always had this stubborn arrogance. Part of it comes from being a Lucas, I guess. My dad was so sure we were a breed apart, and some of it rubbed off on me. We always seem to need to reinforce how special we are — even more than we need to explain our actions or, God forbid, apologize for anything to anybody!"

There was silence again. Scott quietly closed the lid of the piano. "I couldn't leave town without seeing you again, Stacey, without saying I'm sorry if you were embarrassed this morning, or if I made you regret the last forty-eight hours." He hesitated. "Fate, coincidence — whatever brought you to the ranch the other night — well, that was the happiest I've been in a long time."

Stacey shivered inwardly with some new, deep understanding of the proud man who had humbled himself to her, and she knew what an effort saying all that had taken. Her heart, in spite of all her resolutions, melted. "You're going away?" she asked in a low voice.

"Yes, but only for a few weeks. When I get back . . ." he hesitated, "can I — can we see each other?"

Stacey looked into those eyes now softened either by a trick of light or a new gentleness and had an almost irresistible urge to kiss him.

She turned away quickly. *Easy, Stacy,* she warned herself. *This is much too fast.* She was not going to fall so easily for someone she still felt so uncertain about. She sought a light touch.

"Of course. I'm at the Sign of the Carousel every day from ten until four," she said smiling.

"I meant, after working hours," he said with a relieved grin.

"I'd like that."

"When I get back, I'll be in touch."

She walked out onto the front porch with him. The twilight was soft with rain.

They said good-bye, and Stacey watched him drive away. When she went back inside, she was humming.

Chapter Thirteen

The idea of having an old-fashioned tree-trimming party came to Stacey one November day when she was rummaging in the attic and came upon a cardboard box of old Christmas ornaments among stacks of ancient copies of *The Saturday Evening Post* and *St. Nicholas* magazines. There were faded paper cornucopias, fragile glass globes, feathered birds to perch with metal clips on tree branches, crystal icicles, and tarnished tinsel ropes; she even found some tiny candle holders from the days when real lighted candles were placed on Christmas trees.

Decorating this lovely old house for Christmas seemed a wonderful plan, and when Stacey shared the idea with Nora, she was enthusiastic.

"There's a tree farm not far from here where you can select, then cut your own tree," Nora told her. "You'll need at least a ten-footer with these high ceilings."

"Great, and we'll do it with all the neat old-fashioned things like cranberry beads and popcorn strings."

"And everyone can bring a homemade ornament or something special for the tree," suggested Nora, warming to the idea.

"We'll have punch —"

"Have everyone bring a batch of cookies."

So the party planning went forth. The Saturday night of the first weekend in December was set, and Stacey sent out invitations which read,

> This night I hold an old accustom'd
>   fest —
> Whereto I have invited many a guest,
> Such as I love, and you among the store.
> One more, most welcome, makes my
>   number more.
>
> Shakespeare

Tree-Trimming Party at the Sign of the
Carousel
Popcorn Stringing, Christmas Carols
Please bring a batch of your favorite
Christmas cookies.

Woodfern had already begun its transformation into merrye old England for Decem-

168

ber. Swags of real greens swung from lamppost to lamppost all down Main Street, their columns festooned with red ribbon and big bows. Store windows were gaily decorated, displaying all kinds of beautiful gifts, crafts, and toys. The clerks were appropriately costumed as were the waitresses and waiters in the various coffee shops, restaurants, and cafes. The whole town had taken on a festive air.

Rehearsals were in progress for the annual performance of Dickens' *A Christmas Carol*, with a benefit opening performance set for the second weekend in December. Val and Shawn were deeply involved, of course, but eager to come to Stacey's party before every weekend would have to be spent on stage.

Stacey had sent Scott an invitation, but since she had not heard from him, she did not know if he would be back in time to come. Amidst all her preparation, a little stirring of hope rose within her that he would suddenly appear on her doorstep.

But the evening of the party arrived, and there had been no word at all from him. "He could at least have sent a postcard," she chided her reflection in the mirror, as she did up her hair, pinned it under, then attached a flat, black velvet bow. Unconsciously she wished he could see her all dressed up for a change, looking feminine and frilly in a scoop-necked, ruffled blouse and a long, crimson, quilted skirt with a wide black cumberbund.

The party was a huge success, and Stacey felt it would have been perfect if only someone else were there. The big, beautiful cedar had been brought in earlier by Paul and Jeff, and its pungent scent filled the house. Stacey had ordered new ornaments from a company that specialized in Victorian reproductions of original ornaments, as she felt the ones she had found were too fragile. And all the guests had contributed delightful individual ones to make the tree sparkle and glow like a picture from an old-fashioned book.

There was much merry chatter and light-hearted conversation as the berries were strung, the popcorn popped, the cookies tasted, and the punch enjoyed. The tree trimming took a long time because of the tree's height and size, and as the decorating progressed each step had to be viewed and admired by all.

At the height of the merriment, the front door bell rang suddenly in several short, impatient pulls. Stacey, who was nearest, ran to open it with an excited hope that it just might be Scott. But when she opened the door it was King Steele who stood glowering at her.

He jerked a thumb in the direction of the road without a word of greeting and growled, "I got the Ranch's four-horse trailer onto my truck, and somebody's Dodge station wagon is parked any which way at your driveway, and it's blocking me gettin' by." His thin lips compressed into a hard line. "Would you get whoever owns it to get it out of my way?"

What a terribly unpleasant man he is! Stacey thought as she recoiled at his rudeness.

"What is it, Stacey?" Shawn had come up behind her.

Stacey turned around, "I believe it must be Fay's station wagon that's at the edge of the drive. It's blocking —" she turned back and gestured toward Steele. "Shawn, this is the Lucas Ranch foreman, King Steele, Shawn Kent —" but she was not able to complete the introduction, for Steele had turned away, saying over his shoulder, "I'll wait in the truck."

"Who did you say that was? Ebenezer Scrooge?" Shawn asked archly. "I'll get Fay's keys and move it for her. She's an awful parker, but then, she can barely reach the pedals and it doesn't have power steering."

That one unpleasant incident hardly marred an otherwise gala evening, Stacey thought, as her guests began to leave. Florin reminded her of his party on the evening of December 23 after the last performance of *A Christmas*

Carol when he would be entertaining the cast and friends at a costume party at his gallery after the show.

When everyone had left, she took all the empty cups, plates, and refreshment leftovers to the kitchen, then turned out all but the Christmas tree lights. She curled up in the window seat and sat for a moment enjoying them.

She felt just a trace of melancholy as she thought of her parents in Belgium, and she wished she had someone special to share this moment with. But it only lasted a minute, for Stacey felt she had too much to be happy about this Christmas to spend any time feeling lonely.

The next few weeks she was busier than she had even imagined she would be. Her Christmas shoppers were discriminating antique hunters who neither blinked nor balked at prices. They were looking for gifts of quality, uniqueness, and value for people who were very dear to them. Even though at the end of the day she was bone tired, Stacey felt a wonderful exuberance at having helped people to find just what they wanted, or having suggested something they had not thought of, or found something they had searched for elsewhere. Almost everyone left the store pleased with their purchases.

The three weeks before Christmas flew by, and all at once it was the night of December 23. Stacey was getting ready to attend the last performance of *A Christmas Carol* and to go on to the party at Florin's gallery. She was going to change into her costume at Aris Brady's house since they lived right in town and near the theater.

Stacey had been too busy to see the play earlier, but it had received rave reviews from everyone who had and she was especially looking forward to seeing it.

As she drove into Woodfern that evening, the nagging disappointment that Scott had failed to write or phone surfaced. "Why should I care so much?" she asked herself crossly. " 'I'll call you' is something everyone says. He might have meant to, even, then changed his mind." It was just that there had seemed to be something — something she couldn't put her finger on — about him that was different. Scott Lucas did not seem to be the kind of person who said meaningless things.

A hubbub of people was thronging the small lobby of Woodfern's Repertory Theater. Stacey was ushered to a seat in an otherwise empty row by a pretty teenager charmingly dressed in the ruffled cap and apron of a Victorian maid.

Stacey looked at the program and saw that Val was playing a dual role as Mrs. Cratchit and the ghost of Christmas past. The house lights dimmed and there was a ripple of anticipation throughout the audience as the curtains parted on the scene of the poor clerk Bob Cratchit hunched over his high desk in the ill-heated office of his employer, Ebenezer Scrooge.

At the same time there was a stir and rustling as a party of late-comers filed into the row where Stacey was seated.

Stacey, who always made it a point to ignore theatergoers with the bad manners to arrive late, focused her eyes and attention on the opening scene of the play. Soon she found herself completely engrossed. The sets, the staging, and the acting were all of professional quality. She mentally congratulated Shawn on his expert direction and applauded Val on her characterization, which had totally transformed the glamorous woman into a plump, cheerful English wifey.

So caught up was she in the delightful if familiar play, beloved from childhood, Stacey was not even aware of the murmurs or movement in the seats next to her — that is, until the lights went on for the intermission and she glanced casually to her right.

A few seats over among the party who had

come in late was Trish Findlay, and beside her sat Scott.

Stacey drew in her breath sharply, then stared straight ahead, trying to compose herself and not show the surprise she felt. So Scott was back! How long had he been back? And why had he not called her? Those questions flooded into her mind as blood rushed into her face. She felt humiliated. She wished desperately she could sink into the seat or the floor or somehow disappear. She heard the shuffling of feet, chair seats being shoved back, as people started moving toward the lobby. At Intermission, it had been announced, wassail, coffee, or spiced cider would be served, and people were flocking up the aisles.

Risking a wary glance to see if the coast was clear, she saw Trish and thought Trish had also seen her. But Trish deliberately turned away, slipping her hand through Scott's arm.

Undecided as to the best way to avoid Scott, Stacey sat for a few minutes collecting herself. Discretion was the better part of valor, she finally concluded, and she could make for the ladies' room and remain there until the lights dimmed again for the second act to begin. It was cowardly but . . .

She rose from her seat and had started up the aisle when she bumped right into Florin.

"I spotted you from the back!" he said,

greeting her. "I was just coming to get you. How are you enjoying the play? Great, isn't it? By the way, there's an empty seat beside me in the tenth row. Would you like to watch the rest of the performance with me?"

He must have been startled by her enthusiastic acceptance, Stacey reflected later, as she sat three rows behind Trish and Scott for the remainder of the performance. But Florin was one of the nicest, most uncomplicated people she had ever known, especially for someone who ran a gallery and dealt with artists all the time. Maybe that was what gave him the air of detached calmness he always exuded.

As the cast was taking a second curtain call Florin excused himself to dash over to the gallery and supervise the last-minute preparations, and Stacey took the opportunity to slip out of the theater and successfully avoid a face-to-face confrontation with Scott. She drove over to the Bradys, who had seen the play the week before and were waiting for her. She made a quick change into her costume, and together they all went over to Florin's gallery.

Florin had decorated the gallery in the style of a street in Dickens' England. With his clever artistic talent, he had evoked the essence of everyone's idealized version of what it must have been like. Vendors' stalls were positioned all around with all sorts of delicious and tempting goodies to sample such as roasting chestnuts, hot stuffed "murphies," pumpkin and mince tarts, individual fruit cakes, and candied apples on sticks along with mulled cider, eggnog, and coffee.

All sorts of games had been set up — including darts and skittles, and a puppet show was going on in one corner. Everyone came in costume, and when the cast members arrived still in theirs, it would have been easy to believe the whole crowd had been magically transported from the England of a century ago.

It was fairly simple for Stacey to lose herself in the milling guests who circulated constantly among an intriguing medley of booths, entertainment, and exhibits. She did not think the Findlay crowd knew Florin or that he would have invited them to this party, so she felt fairly sure she would not run into Scott.

She was examining a display of dolls with dried-apple faces dressed as famous Victorian characters when she heard that deep, familiar voice behind her.

"Stacey!"

She whirled around and found herself practically in Scott's arms.

He looked incredibly handsome in a high-collared, ruffled shirt, wide cravat, and swallow-tailed buff coat.

" 'Little Nell of Old Curiosity Shop,' I presume," he said in his teasing way.

She felt her face flush but tried to remain poised. She gave him an arch look. "Steerforth or Squeers?" she asked coolly.

He frowned. "You're angry."

"Angry? Why should I be angry?" she said indifferently.

"Let me explain."

"Oh, please, don't bother. Remember, never explain. Your friends don't need it, and your enemies don't believe it anyway. There's nothing to explain."

She started to move past him, holding her wide-skirted dress to sweep by, but he caught her arm.

"Wait, Stacey. I just got back in town this afternoon. I've been on a ranch in Montana, miles from anywhere. Even if I'd written — which I really didn't have time to — but even if I had, it would still not have reached you."

"You don't have to explain anything to me, Scott," Stacey said again.

"But I do. I want to. Driving to the play tonight, I hoped I might see you. I went by the house, but it was all dark so I knew you weren't there. You see, the Findlays bought a whole block of tickets for the performance. Mr. Findlay likes to think of himself as a patron of the arts. Anyway, Trish called to say they have a houseful of guests from the city for the holidays and she wanted me to join them. That's how I happened to come to the play and to this party, on the chance that I'd see you."

She hesitated. Looking up into those penetrating blue eyes, she almost believed him. She wanted to believe him.

"Look, all the way back on the plane today I kept thinking about you. I was hoping that I'd be seeing you soon. Don't turn me off like that, please."

"Oh, there you are!" Another voice, also familiar — a little high, a little shrill — broke the moment. Stacey turned her head slightly and saw Trish Findlay, looking delightful in a pink satin costume, all frothy ruffles and velvet bows.

" 'Dora Copperfield' in the flesh," murmured Stacey.

"Or Ebenezer's first love!" dimpled Trish, fluttering a lace fan coquettishly. "Isn't this too much! Florin is so clever, isn't he? I brought Daddy in to buy some paintings for his office, Scott, and Florin is so intelligent and charming!" As she spoke she slipped her arm through Scott's. "Scott, come along, I'm famished. They have the most marvelous food over there."

"You go ahead. I'll join you in a minute,"

Scott told her evenly but firmly.

Trish gave him and Stacey an icy glare, but went.

Scott said, "Stacey, I have to socialize a little with these people, but may I take you home?"

"I have my own car here, thank you."

"Then may I follow you home?"

"It's awfully late —"

"Not too late," he countered. "At least, I *hope* it's not too late."

"I don't know."

"Stacey, we've got to talk. There's so much I want to tell you. About my trip, and about some things I've been thinking. Come on, give me a chance?"

"Well —"

"Can you leave in about a half-hour?"

"Gracefully? Yes, I guess." She gave a reluctant smile.

"I'll have to come in this ridiculous outfit," he said with a grin.

"It will be perfect in my house," she said finally, knowing she was giving in — knowing it and suddenly not caring.

Chapter Fourteen

An hour later they were seated at Stacey's kitchen table smiling at each other over mugs of steaming cocoa.

"So, how was your trip?" Stacey asked.

Scott looked serious. "Very educational," he said in a professorial manner. "I learned a lot that will help if I decide to go ahead with my experiment."

"Experiment?"

"Raising llamas — on a big scale, I mean. Last year I started with six — three males and three females. I had read a great deal about them, seen them in their native habitat in Peru, and talked to ranchers in South America. I was intrigued with the idea of raising them. But there's a ban on importing them. So I had to find out where they were being raised successfully in North America. Outside of zoos, of course."

"They do seem like a kind of exotic animal," Stacey said thoughtfully.

"That's because most Americans are not used to seeing them grazing peacefully in pastures here, and it explodes a widespread myth about llamas. The theory that they have to live at extremely high altitudes just doesn't fit the facts. The unique thing about llamas is that they can adapt to almost any environment, even sea level."

"Is all this — raising llamas — something that's happened just recently?"

"In part, although in the twenties a man named Lindemann in New York became interested in llamas through his father, a zoologist, and set up a breeding preserve in the Catskill Mountains. And William Randolph Hearst, when he was building his castle estate, San Simeon, thought llamas would be just the thing to see browsing on the craggy cliffs above the ocean in southern California. So he brought some in, too. But that was more or less his desire to collect rare things in nature as well as art treasures."

"I don't want to seem dumb, but do they, the llamas, have any real purpose, that is, other than their strangeness?"

"They are tireless pack animals," Scott told her. "And although at the present time there's no major market for their wool in the United States, the Peruvians have been using it for centuries."

"They seem almost as though they'd make good pets," Stacey said with a smile, remembering feeding the baby llama the night of the storm.

"Oh, they're fabulous — gentle, good-natured — they respond to humans to a fantastic degree. For the rancher they have many desirable qualities. They are practically disease-free, require no shots or hoof-trimming, and subsist on a minimum amount of feed." Scott took a long sip of cocoa, put down his mug, and said, "In short, there are so many rewarding possibilities in raising them over the conventional ranching of cattle or sheep, that I —" he broke off suddenly. "Hey! I've been talking nonstop! I bet I've been boring you."

"No, I'm really intrigued," Stacey said honestly.

Scott gave her a look that was a mixture of skepticism and awe. "Most women would have been bored by now."

"Not me. Scout's honor." She held up her right hand in the familiar salute.

Suddenly Scott leaned across the table and kissed her on the mouth.

She blinked, startled, and he smiled mischievously. "Mmmm, you taste like chocolate. My favorite flavor."

She recovered herself enough to stand up.

"Then, you must want some more cocoa."

He got up, too, shaking his head.

"No. It's late. I don't want to outstay my welcome after inviting myself over."

They walked out of the kitchen, along the passageway to the front hall. Scott looked into the parlor where the Christmas tree stood in the bay window. Stacey had left its lights on, and the myriad colors danced on the ceiling, the walls, and were reflected on the glass of the window. Turning his head slowly, he took in the stairway where Stacey had twisted evergreen boughs and red satin ribbon around the polished newel post, and the twin holly wreaths on the double front doors.

"This is a beautiful house," Scott said quietly, and his glance moved to include her. Looking at her as if admiring a painting, his eyes swept from her hair, held back by a wide, blue velvet band and cascading onto her shoulders, to her prim, high-necked calico dress and pinafore, then rested with infinite tenderness on her face. He added, "And you grace it beautifully."

Momentarily taken aback by this unexpected gallantry, Stacey dropped a demure curtsy and shyly said, "Thank you kindly, sir."

He smiled at her indulgently, then took her hand, and together they walked out onto the porch where a pale winter moon had just crested the tree tops.

They stood in the moonlight silently for a minute. Stacey shivered slightly, more from a kind of inner excitement than cold, and almost instinctively Scott put his arm around her shoulder. She looked at him, wondering if he would kiss her good night. Did she want him to? Her question was answered simply as Scott's strong fingers gently cupped her chin and raised it. He bent and kissed her softly on the mouth.

Stacey's heart stirred, and she was touched with a thrilling little tremble she could not remember ever having felt before. It was almost as if something wonderful were about to happen.

Then Scott drew her into his arms and held her for a long time, his chin resting on the top of her head. After a while he released her, held her by the shoulders, and kissed her again lightly.

"Good night, 'Little Nell,'" he said, chuckling. Then his tall figure was down the steps and striding through the gate. It squeaked as he opened it.

"You ought to get that fixed," he called back, laughing. Watching him go, Stacey laughed, too. It had been a long time since she had felt such happiness. She stood watching him drive off. He had the top down on his sports car and the moonlight had turned his hair a glistening silver.

How extraordinary this evening had turned out, how different from what she had at first thought it would be! She went inside, then shut and locked the door.

Scott was so different from what she had thought him to be! She wanted to know so much more about him. She hoped tonight was the beginning of many more conversations and shared experiences. More than ever, now, she wanted to explore the many facets of his personality. But she was *not*, she promised herself, *repeat, not,* going to plunge headlong into an impulsive romance. *She'd had enough of that.* She was going to keep her head, no matter how magical tonight had seemed!

All of Christmas week seemed magical — from the candlelight service at the church on Christmas Eve, where Scott's magnificent rendition of "O Holy Night" sent tingling sensations through Stacey and moved many in the congregation to wipe away a few tears, to Christmas Day spent with Nora and Jeff. Stacey experienced only a tiny twinge of homesickness for her own family as the group who had become her friends held hands around the festive Christmas dinner table and gave thanks.

The dinner was a farewell party as well, because Fay was leaving within a few days to spend the rest of the winter painting in Mexico. She promised to bring many finished works to hang in Florin's gallery in the spring. Shawn and Val were heading for an extended vacation in the East, where both their families lived, and to take in the Broadway season of plays.

"It's going to be a ghost town around here after the holidays," complained Stacey as the group discussed their plans. Even Florin was closing the gallery for a few weeks to visit some exhibits in Los Angeles, Carmel, and San Francisco.

"I'm also going to spend a few days in Mendocino," he told the group. "The art center there is showing some exciting new artists."

"Mendocino! I've heard so much about it, but I've never been there," Stacey remarked.

"You should go. It's just off the beaten track enough to avoid the commercialism of Carmel and some of the crowds. But it's worth taking the extra time between here and the city to stop for a day or two," Florin commented.

Holiday activities in Woodfern also included a midnight buffet supper party held at the Findlays, to which Stacey was not invited, and a New Year's Day open house at the Townsends', to which she was.

But most memorable of all was New Year's Eve. Scott had a vivid crimson amaryllis plant delivered to Stacey on Christmas Eve afternoon with a card saying, "Save New Year's Eve for me." He had called her Christmas morning before she left for the Phillips's. They made plans then to have dinner together "somewhere special."

The amaryllis was still beautifully blooming on December 31, and as Stacey got ready for the evening ahead, she found she was looking forward to seeing Scott with a kind of tremulous excitement.

Her freshly shampooed hair kept slipping out of the pins as she tried to sweep it up into a French roll, so she let it fall loosely, held on either side with the cloisonné combs her brother had sent her for Christmas. She wore a soft wool dress, the color of hyacinths.

She was just coming down the stairs when she saw a man walk up on the porch. To her surprise it was Larry Meade.

When she opened the door she noticed two things. It was drizzling outside, and under his raincoat Larry was dressed for a formal evening.

"Merry Christmas and Happy New Year!" he greeted her jovially.

"What a nice surprise! Come in," she said.

He stepped inside. "I can only stay a minute." He flashed her a rather self-conscious grin and flipped his bow tie with an extravagant gesture. "As you may have noted, I'm on my way to a gala New Year's Eve celebration — the annual Volunteer Firemen's ball. It's held at the civic auditorium, thank goodness, so I don't have to drive far. It looks like it's going to be one of those typical northern California winter nights. Fog's already rolling in."

Stacey offered him a cup of coffee, but he shook his head. "No, sorry, I've got to be on my way to pick up my date." He reached into the deep pocket of his raincoat as he said, "I just wanted to bring by something that belongs to you, or to your great-aunt Eustacia Valentine, actually. I guess as her heir they come to you. I found these when I accidentally hit a hidden spring in the old desk I bought from you and discovered a secret drawer behind one of the pigeonholes." He pulled out a packet of envelopes, tied with a faded blue ribbon, and handed them to Stacey. "Letters, I'd say."

"Why, thank you, Larry," Stacey said, looking at the small stack of square letters addressed in a round, almost childish handwriting to "Miss Eustacia Valentine, Rt. 2, Woodfern, California."

"Are you sure you won't have some coffee?" she asked again.

Larry had his hand on the doorknob. "I'd like to, but no thanks. You must be getting ready to go out yourself. You certainly look smashing."

She found herself blushing.

"Well, yes, and you'd probably never guess with whom."

Larry raised his eyebrows, questioningly.

"Scott Lucas," she told him, knowing he would hear about it sooner or later.

The eyebrows went up higher. He shrugged. "Well, I guess there's more than one way to skin a cat, as they say." Then he winced. "I've always hated that expression. Don't know why I used it."

"Slipped out, didn't it?" Stacey laughed. "I gather you have some reservations about my seeing Scott socially?"

"Well," Larry dragged the word out slowly, "not that it's hard to understand why any guy in his right mind wouldn't like to go out with you. You're bright, charming, attractive — beautiful, in fact. It's just that maybe I don't trust Scott's motives. After all, he was after your property, remember."

"Is that any way to talk about your old school chum?" she asked, half joking, half serious.

"I'm your lawyer, too, Stacey, don't forget. And the nature of the breed is to be suspicious of young men who come courting heiresses!"

"I'd hardly call myself an heiress! A white elephant of an old house that needs all sorts of repairs, a few acres of land —"

"Land values in this state have skyrocketed in the last few years," Larry said matter-of-factly. "Scott's no fool. He may have just figured another way around getting hold of some valuable property."

"You're a cynic, Larry!"

"You're right. Forgive me. I hope I haven't spoiled your evening. I guess I just recall that Scott's always had young women vying for his attention. He's considered quite a romantic figure and —" he stopped abruptly as if he had changed his mind about what he was going to say. "Good night, Stacey, and Happy New Year, again. Enjoy!" he called over his shoulder as he went out into the rainy night.

Stacey took the packet of letters into her combination sitting room and office. She sat down in one of the plush upholstered rockers in front of the corner brick-and-tile fireplace and studied the envelope on the top of the pile. Although the ink was badly faded, she was able to read the return address: "Lt. R. T. Lucas, Somewhere in France." She bent to read the date on the postmark and made out a dim "1918." Slowly it dawned on Stacey that Lt. R. T. Lucas must be the Rollin Lucas to whom the stained-glass window in the Community Church was dedicated, and he had written these letters to her great-aunt!

Stacey held the packet for a long time, debating whether or not she should read one or two. It seemed an invasion of privacy and yet something strongly prompted her to read them. It seemed too much of a coincidence that these letters from another Lucas man to her own relative should come into her possession just now. Maybe these letters had something to tell her — something Great-Aunt Eustacia wanted her to know.

Slowly Stacey untied the frayed ribbon and opened the first envelope. They were in sequence, and the first letter had been written on the troop ship going overseas. She gathered from what he said that he and Eustacia had known each other from childhood and had been high-school sweethearts. The words were full of bravado and staunch determination to be a courageous soldier, but here and there were nostalgic bits of remembrance.

Stacey could not help herself. One letter followed the other, and she read on, fascinated by the growing maturity in the letters as Rollin reached France and began fighting. His letters to Eustacia continued boyishly dear and sentimental, assuring her of his love, speaking of the things they had done together that last summer and the things he longed to do with her in the future.

The last letter in the bunch spoke of a coming big offensive he had heard was just ahead. It ended by telling her he loved her and hoped "all this will be over soon and we can be riding through Lucas Valley together again next summer."

Just when Aunt Eustacia had received the news of his death, there was no indication, but a yellowed newspaper clipping with his picture and the caption "KILLED IN ACTION, COUNTY FAMILY LOSES SON IN BATTLE OF MARNE" was with the letters, along with another clipping dated some years later. It was the famous World War I poem, "In Flanders Field."

So that is why Great-Aunt Eustacia never married, Stacey thought, as she refolded all the letters and tied them back together. Eustacia had been in love with Rollin Lucas. Perhaps they had even been secretly engaged before he went overseas. She had gone on mourning her lost love, collecting things she would never use, buying more and more until she had rooms bursting with things she had planned to share with him.

How sad, and yet how romantic, in a way.

Her love had lasted all those years. No one else could take the place of the man she had committed her love to.

The sound of the front doorbell startled Stacey and brought her back from the dreamy past. She felt happiness sweep over her as she went to open the door for another Lucas come courting.

Chapter Fifteen

At the sight of Scott, all of Larry Meade's comments vanished from Stacey's consciousness. A kind of euphoria took over as she welcomed him out of the chill and into the warmth of the house. It had begun to rain in earnest, and as she led him into her sitting room, he rubbed his hands together appreciatively and walked over to the fire.

With a thick Irish brogue he said, "Shure 'tis not a fit night out for man nor beast."

Stacey clapped her hands. "Bravo! I believe you missed your calling, Scott. You should have gone on the stage."

"I almost did," he replied and turned and looked into the fire thoughtfully.

"You did?" Stacey's curiosity was piqued.

"Well, you might say I was toying with the idea. When I was at prep school, I was in the drama group. We put on plays and musicals. I liked the musicals best." He turned back, smiling broadly. "I had the role of the admiral in Gilbert and Sullivan's *H. M. S. Pinafore.*"

"My goodness, I *am* impressed. Does Shawn Kent know? Probably not, or you'd be in his next production." Stacey smiled.

Scott shook his head. "No, when I came back to Woodfern I put on a different hat. A rancher's hat. My dad took a dim view of the theatrical life." He brushed his hands as if symbolically dusting off any lingering touch of that part of his life.

Although she was curious, Stacey could see Scott did not want to discuss it further. A sudden burst of rain diverted their attention for the moment. They looked at each other significantly as they heard the clatter of rain on the tin roof of the back porch, which ran the length of the house.

"Listen to that!" Stacey declared. "Another nor'wester'?"

"Maybe *I'll* get stranded *here* this time!" suggested Scott with a wicked gleam in his eyes.

"In the meantime," Stacey said pointedly, "would you like something to drink? Cocoa? Coffee?"

"Coffee sounds great."

She started toward the kitchen and he followed her. "By the way, I didn't make reservations anywhere. I'm not sure why, except that most people around here have home parties on New Year's Eve, and I didn't think we'd have any problem getting a table at the Lamplighter. I hope that wasn't a mistake."

It struck Stacey as odd that someone as organized as Scott seemed to be had not made reservations. But on the other hand, the idea of going out on New Year's Eve had never appealed to her. All those people wearing funny hats, blowing horns, drinking too much, and trying desperately to be happy, either to forget a past unhappy year or not to admit their dread that the next year would be as bad. Those public celebrations always struck her as sadly phony.

Scott's broad-shouldered figure seemed to fill up the kitchen. Trinket jumped out of her box near the stove and gave a tentative bark. Scott squatted down on his heels and called her gently. The stump of a tail wagged hesitantly and then she scampered toward him. He scratched her chest and rubbed behind her ears and she wiggled all over. He looked up at Stacey. "What's her name?"

"Trinket," Stacey answered.

"Suits," he said.

"I don't think I know what your Lab's name is either," she said as she filled the kettle with water.

"Troy," Scott replied. Then he grinned. "Trinket and Troy. These two should get to know each other. They could become friends."

"After a bad beginning —"

"Well, we did, didn't we?" He stood, thrust his hands in his pockets and looked around. "This is a great kitchen, a real down-home kind of kitchen, not all sterile and chrome. This kitchen has character."

"I love it," Stacey said. "I can see why in the old days a kitchen was considered the heart of a home."

Outside, the sound of the rain became even louder. It sounded as if it were not going to let up. Stacey thrust more kindling into the little wood stove and poked the fire into a blaze. She got out the lovely blue and white cups and saucers from the pine hutch and put them on the table.

She paused for a second, then said, "I don't know what you'd think of this idea, but . . . why not just fix something here to eat tonight rather than going out?"

"What? Did I hear right?" Scott looked shocked. "You mean you don't want to go out to some glamorous place to see in the New Year?"

"You forget I lived in San Francisco for two years and practically every time I went out to eat it was to a glamorous place." She laughed and made a sweeping movement with both hands. "Now, a place like this would be a real find in the city! I mean, people would flock here and tell their friends of the unique place they'd discovered."

"I guess you're right. It all depends on your viewpoint," Scott agreed. "But are you sure? I mean, I planned —" He frowned. "Scratch that! I guess I didn't plan very well."

"If you'll be satisfied with leftovers," Stacey said, going over to look into the refrigerator.

"Wait! Hold everything! Since you've provided the place, the least I can do is provide the meal." Scott took off his jacket, hung it on the back of one of the chairs, and rolled up his sleeves.

"Now let's see, have you got eggs, milk, bread, butter, and cinnamon?"

Stacey, her hands on her hips, looked puzzled. "What are you going to make, or is it bake?"

Scott regarded her in mock astonishment. "Don't you know the ingredients of one of the international gourmet delicacies? The test of the expertise of the great chefs of Europe?"

"A souffle?"

"Don't try me too far, madam," he said severely. "No, but you were close. French toast," he said with a flair.

Stacey brought out a bowl of fresh brown eggs, a carton of milk, sugar, a loaf of bread, and rummaged in one of the cabinets for cinnamon.

"You make the coffee, and I'll get to work," Scott directed as he deftly started greasing the large, square, cast iron skillet.

Soon the combined odors of coffee, cinnamon, and the pine scent from the snapping wood fire blended deliciously. Outside, the downpour drummed on the roof, increasing the feeling of intimacy within.

Finally everything was ready. A linen cloth banded with blue cross-stitching covered the table, which Stacey had set with the rest of the Blue Willow china, and Scott triumphantly brought a platter of fluffy toast, delicately browned and sprinkled with cinnamon, and placed it in the center. He stepped back. "Voilà!"

"Congratulations!" Stacey held up her hand making a circle with her index finger and thumb. "They look perfect!"

"The true test is in the taste," Scott assured her, holding out a chair for her to be seated. Stacey had provided honey, maple syrup, and creamy butter to top the squares of toast, and for a minute they were silent as they each took a first bite.

Stacey closed her eyes and sighed. "Delicious!"

"Now you see I have hidden talents," Scott

announced proudly, forking a bite and smiling mischievously. "It would be to your advantage to check out the rest of them."

"To think I never dreamed you could cook!" Stacey widened her eyes dramatically as though aghast at the thought.

"It would have changed your impression of me drastically, right?"

Her mouth full, she nodded.

"Of course, I should tell you right off before you get any ideas — I don't do windows."

They both laughed. Scott leaned back in his chair and looked at her. "This was a wonderful idea. I don't remember having this much fun on New Year's Eve before. Usually I'm trying too hard to give the impression that I am!"

When they had finished they took their coffee cups and went into the sitting room. The fire was glowing and the steady beat of the rain continued outside. They sat together on the sofa, and Stacey told Scott about finding the letters from his great-uncle to her great-aunt.

"It was almost like reading one of the great classic love stories," she said softly, gazing into the fire pensively.

"I suspect you're incurably romantic."

Stacey defended herself. "Is there something wrong with that?"

"No, it's just that it's rare. Most people, by the time they're grown up, have been disillusioned of the very idea of true love." He paused, then asked quizzically. "Do you actually believe love lasts? I mean the kind that is all-consuming and takes over your life?"

"Yes, I do. I think it can," Stacey said firmly.

Scott raised an eyebrow. "Fifteen months. That's what the experts say, you know. Even the grandest passion only can last a little more than a year."

Stacey shook her head vigorously.

"I don't believe that. Not for a minute. My parents are living proof that two people can go on loving each other for thirty years or longer. My brother and I have always felt that even though they were great parents, they really didn't need anyone else to be happy."

Scott was quiet for a moment, then speaking slowly, he nodded his head. "Maybe, for some lucky few, it happens. My father adored my mother. He was never the same after she died."

A silence fell between them. The pelting rain and the occasional sizzle of a burning log provided a background to their separate, unspoken thoughts.

Watching him, Stacey thought, *Someone has hurt him badly. Down deep he isn't as cynical or as invulnerable as he would like people to think.*

When they began to talk again they spoke of other things — of Europe, of where they had been, of special memories and times spent in mutually familiar places. They agreed that San Francisco was the most "European" of American cities, with its many different cultures, its international flavor, and its ethnic restaurants.

They were both startled when the banjo clock on the wall above the mantlepiece began slowly striking midnight.

"I can't believe it!" exclaimed Stacey, starting to get up. "I don't even have anything to toast in the New Year!"

"Never mind! I should have thought of it. I just hope all the traditional things I didn't do this evening don't mean some kind of omen for the year ahead for me." Scott reached out and circled her wrist with his hand. Their eyes held, and the clock went on striking.

Scott stood up and drew her gently, deliberately, into his arms. He gazed down into her eyes, a smile softening the angles and planes of his face. "Happy New Year, Stacey Thornton," he murmured as he bent to her. She closed her eyes, hearing her heart beat in accompaniment to the rhythmic drumming of the rain, feeling all her defenses against falling in love with Scott melt away in a joyous response to the tender intensity of his kiss.

A few moments later, arms around each other's waists, they walked to the front door. Stacey leaned her head against Scott's shoulder, experiencing a floating sensation that seemed not quite real.

At the door he pulled her to him again, hugging her close. Her cheek was pressed against the rough tweed of his jacket, and one of the leather buttons felt uncomfortably hard on her skin. But she did not want to move.

"Words sometimes spoil things, don't you think?" he whispered huskily. "Let me just say this New Year's Eve has been very special."

Before he left, he kissed her again, and as he was going out the door he said, "I'll pick you up around four to go to Leta Townsend's open house, O.K.?"

Stacey stayed awake until three in the morning. At least, that was the time when she last looked at her bedside clock. She felt as if she must be dreaming. Would she wake up the next morning and find that it all had been a dream — that Scott had never kissed her nor held her and said all those things?

But when he arrived the next afternoon exactly at four, bringing her another single red rose, Stacey realized it was not a dream but something exciting and beautiful that had begun to happen.

When they arrived at the Townsends' house, Leta's sharp eyes darted back and forth between Stacey and Scott. Leta, who prided herself on never missing a thing, realized immediately that there was something different about Scott. And she observed a brightness about Stacey — a new sparkle in her dark-lashed eyes, a softness about her mouth, a heightened color on her face.

Leta regarded them both with eyes lively and dancing with curiosity, but she waited to get Stacey alone before saying anything else.

Stacey had never been inside the Townsend house before, and she enjoyed the spacious, almost formal atmosphere that seemed to contrast with Leta's rather blunt personality. Stacey's now-trained eye spotted some beautiful French antiques mingling harmoniously with comfortable contemporary armchairs and sofas covered in bright polished chintz. Leta still had her Christmas decorations up, which lent a sophisticated gaiety to the rooms. The tree was covered with white and gold balls, and white poinsettia plants were everywhere. An elegant buffet was spread on an exquisitely appointed table in the adjoining dining room.

Stacey recognized most of the other guests.

If she had not met them through friends, she recognized them and they her from having been to the Carousel. She found it amazingly easy to engage in conversations with people who had been strangers only a few months ago and was secretly amused that she was now considered an antique expert. Everyone seemed to have a question about something they owned or were looking for.

Scott who, of course, knew everybody, circulated with his usual confidence. Every once in a while Stacey caught a glimpse of him across the room and felt her heart give a happy little leap. If he happened at the same time to look her way, and their eyes met, an electric contact tingled between them.

As the crowd thinned, those who were left seemed to gravitate around the piano, where Leta seated herself and began to play. Stacey was astonished at her skill, and Fred beamed happily, inordinately proud of his wife's talent. She moved easily into some of the more familiar show tunes and ballads, and at her urging, Scott began to sing. Others joined in, but it was his strong, sure, true voice that led them. Almost as if on cue, Leta started a medley from *Camelot*, and Stacey sensed an inner thrill as Scott sang.

He was standing directly opposite her on the other side of the piano and he looked right into her eyes as he sang. Suddenly it was as if she and Scott were alone in the room. Even the piano music faded into the distance, and the people around them dimmed into a faint haze. All that seemed to exist was Scott's voice, his eyes, and her feeling of drowning in their depths.

Stacey was not sure when Leta stopped playing. She only became aware of Scott standing next to her, his fingers touching her elbow, and whispering, "Let's get out of here."

But when she went to the bedroom where she had left her coat, Leta followed, came in, closed the door behind her, then confronted Stacey with a twinkle in her eyes.

"Well, young lady, Woodfern seems to agree with you. You're positively blooming. You have the look of love about you. Don't deny it. I've seen it too often to be mistaken."

In spite of herself, Stacey felt a blush suffuse her cheeks. She turned from the mirror of the dressing table, unaware of what a charming picture she made.

"Of course, I'm in love! With my life here, my store, my friends, and Woodfern!"

"*And* Scott Lucas." Leta's statement made denial foolish.

"Maybe. Well, yes. I think so," Stacey said uncertainly. Leta folded her arms across her chest and demanded, "Why do you think you love Scott?"

Stacey took a long moment before answering. Somehow her answer was important, not so much to satisfy Leta as herself. "Because, he's strong, determined, imaginative, and because he's willing to dare something new. I admire that. He's like me, in a way, not being afraid to try something because there's a risk in it. He's got a sense of adventure. That appeals to me. I think we're — a lot alike."

"That's good, but it's not enough to make a good marriage," Leta said firmly.

"Who's talking about marriage?"

"Scott's over thirty. It's time he married, whether he's realized it or not. He almost made a bad mistake — but that's another story." Leta dismissed that and went on. "I like you, Stacey. I did right off. I wouldn't like to see you get hurt."

Leta's remark echoed the warning Larry Meade had made about Scott on New Year's Eve. Unconsciously, Stacey bristled.

"Don't worry about me, Leta. I'm a big girl. Scott isn't the first man I've been attracted to, and I'm still single." Stacey tried to sound casual.

"But Scott Lucas isn't like any other man you've ever known, Stacey. Scott is one of a kind. Loving him could be dangerous."

Stacey picked up her coat and handbag with studied nonchalance, then said, "Thanks, Leta. I know you mean well, but I'll have to make up my own mind about Scott."

With that she gave the older woman a hasty hug and went past her out of the room. She hurried down the hall to where Scott was talking with Fred Townsend by the front door.

They went outside into the crisp, cold air on a night swept clear of rain and fog, and Leta's troubling opinions disappeared like mist in the warmth of Scott's embrace.

"I've been longing all evening to do this," he breathed as he covered her mouth with a kiss that was both tender and intense.

They were in his car with only the dashboard lights illuminating the interior. Stacey could not see his face except in shadow. Still, his kiss seemed to tell her all she needed to know. She felt him take the combs out of her hair and his fingers tangle in its silky waves. She felt them on the nape of her neck, moving with gentle pressure up and down. His face was against her hair and he murmured something she could not hear. Then he was kissing her again and it did not matter.

To Stacey there seemed a certain inevitability to what was happening. It was as if this had all been meant to be — her coming to Woodfern, meeting Scott — everything! She had to believe it was more than happenstance, more than coincidence — it had to be divine coincidence!

His lips were warm on hers once more.

"Scott! Scott!" she heard herself whisper as her arms circled his neck.

Chapter Sixteen

Stacey awoke to the sound of rain. Turning her head toward the window she saw it streaming down the panes. Drowsily she remembered someone telling her that in this part of California it sometimes rained steadily for "forty days and forty nights." In this third week of January the prediction was coming true. Stacey dragged herself out of bed. Almost every day since New Year's Eve it had rained for some part of the day or night.

With a peculiar lack of energy, an intangible feeling of depression, she dressed and went downstairs to the kitchen. She made coffee and stared out the window at the dismal landscape. Wind was whipping the bare branches of the trees along the driveway in a kind of macabre dance, and the rain showed no signs of letting up.

She had read somewhere that the best and quickest remedy for depression was action.

Today, she decided, she would tackle unpacking those two barrels of china Paul had brought in from the barn when he and Jan were deciding what furniture they would take for their Bed and Breakfast Inn.

There was no valid reason for her depression. The last few weeks had been excitingly happy for her, Stacey reminded herself. She and Scott had seen each other at least three times a week since New Year's — walking the deserted beach and combing the dunes for driftwood washed in by the tide, talking, listening to music by firelight, and sharing bits and pieces of their lives.

Almost without her realizing it, their lives were becoming more and more closely intertwined. Was it love, or at least the beginning of love? Their relationship was different from any Stacey had yet had with a man, and by its very uniqueness it made her unsure. She had promised herself never to be swept away again by mere emotion or physical attraction. Without wanting either Larry Meade's or Leta Townsend's warning to make her wary of her own feelings about Scott, Stacey nonetheless found them coming to mind often.

Dredging up all her reluctant energies, Stacey pried off the top of the first barrel and delved into the mounds of excelsior. There was little chance of being interrupted because

212

of the weather and because all business in Woodfern had come to a virtual standstill since Christmas. The Carousel had not had a single customer in days.

The china she began to unpack was Irish Belleek. Its creamy translucency, its eggshell thinness, and the delicacy of its shape and design were among the most beautiful of any of the fine china Stacey had discovered among her aunt's belongings. To find a complete dinner set with twelve place settings plus serving pieces, all in pristine condition, was an unbelievable treasure.

By the time Stacey had reached the bottom of the barrel there was excelsior all over the place and she was hot, dusty, and disheveled. She decided she would carefully wash and then shelve the set in one of the china cabinets before taking a shower and changing out of her jeans and old plaid shirt.

But before she had a chance to do either, the front doorbell rang sharply. Stacey brushed back her straggling hair with her arm, unknowingly wiping a dirty streak across her forehead and cheek. As she went to answer the door she hoped fervently it wasn't Scott. More probably it was Nora.

It turned out to be neither. Instead, Trish Findlay, looking as though she had just had her hair done, a facial, and a massage was standing there. Her outfit was perfection, consisting of a belted, sky-blue raincoat, its collar turned up fetchingly, an Irish-knit tam rakishly set on one side of her head with her dark hair curling out and around it, and a matching scarf flung debonairly over her shoulders.

"Hello there!" she greeted Stacey with ingratiating sweetness. "I hope I'm not disturbing you. The sign says ten to four! I've been dying to come over on a day when it wasn't too crowded to really look around. I want to buy a very special gift."

Trish's brightness put Stacey at a disadvantage. She felt scattered and disoriented by this confident candy-box beauty so in charge of the situation. Her mind tumbled chaotically. Why had Trish Findlay decided to come today? She must have an ulterior reason. Why would she want to buy a special gift here at the Carousel when she probably had charge cards from Bloomingdales, Neiman-Marcus, and Gorgio's of Beverly Hills? But there was nothing else Stacey could do but step back, open the door wider, and say, "Of course. I just didn't think anyone — but, yes, sure, the store hours are —" Her voice trailed off. She felt too awkward in the face of the other woman's composure to act naturally.

"I've just been unpacking china," she said

unnecessarily as the evidence lay all about.

"Oh, do go right ahead with whatever it was you were doing. I'll just browse around and see if I can find anything that appeals to me. Maybe an old-fashioned shaving mug or a pipe rack or a tobacco canister . . ."

Trish had made her point succinctly, Stacey thought, as she began gathering up excelsior from the floor. She was shopping for a man. Her father? Hardly. Clarence Findlay ordered his clothes from a San Francisco tailor who used English and Scottish tweeds and wool exclusively, she was sure. He, too, had access to all or any of the fine accessories and antiques of both countries, since the Findlays went to Europe twice a year. No, Trish Findlay had come to the Carousel today on an errand of her own that had nothing to do with gift buying. Of that, Stacey felt reasonably sure.

After ten minutes or so of prowling around among the tables and chairs in the front display room, picking up various objects and examining them cursorily, then replacing them, Trish ambled over to where Stacey was working. She stopped, quiet for a moment, her long fingernails drumming a tattoo on a polished table top.

"You've really done a fabulous job in this old place. It's delightful. When we were kids we all used to be afraid of this house. It was spooky, you know! We'd ride by here and try to scare each other by saying we saw ghosts in the windows and crazy stuff like that." She gave a little laugh, then continued. "Scott has been telling me about what you've done here and urging me to come and have a look around."

At the mention of Scott's name Stacey unconsciously stiffened. She knew instinctively that Trish was on a "fishing expedition." Bringing up Scott's name was a deliberate device. Now she tensed, waiting to see where Trish was going to go with it.

She did not have to wait long.

"I guess you've been seeing a lot of Scott lately," Trish said. "*We* certainly haven't. I mean, he's usually over at our ranch a lot when he's in Woodfern. But when he decides to go after something he really concentrates on the objective."

Stacey went on pushing the excelsior back into the barrel, making no comment. Trish rushed on.

"My father admires that kind of determination — the kind Scott has. What Daddy doesn't realize is that Scott has other qualities as well." She gave a depreciatory laugh. "That fatal Lucas charm. He is so sincere you'd declare he meant every word he said.

It's only afterward you realize you've been had!" Again she laughed. "Daddy says all the Lucases have had that killer instinct. They go for the jugular. Scott's father was the same way. He outbid my father a number of times for a piece of property or a horse. Dad's smart, too, but not a match for a Lucas."

Stacey's heartbeat began skidding unevenly inside her. Her hands had turned to ice. What was Trish getting at?

"You know, Scott always wanted this property. The land beyond your barn is perfect for extra pastureland. I've never seen him so furious as when you first came here." Trish spoke sharply, as if she wanted some reaction from Stacey. "The fact that you weren't willing to sell it to him really angered him. But, then, Scott has always worked on the theory, 'don't get mad, get even.' "

At this remark Stacey turned her head and looked directly at Trish, wondering what was behind all her chatter. But before she could puzzle it out, Trish continued. Almost as if she were thinking out loud, she said, "Well, I guess I really should have Scott along to help me choose from so many patterns of china and crystal. After all, a wedding selection is terribly important." She let that hit the mark before she added, as she started walking toward the door, "Maybe we should look in the city before we make up our minds definitely. He's driving me down at the end of the week so we'll have time to shop before the wedding."

The closing of the front door echoed through the suddenly quiet house. Dismay clutched Stacey's heart painfully as the gist of Trish's words hit her. Why should she let those careless remarks upset her? Why should she care? They were designed specifically to hurt her, to sow seeds of doubt. But how much of it was true?

After all, long before Stacey had come into the picture, Scott and Trish had known each other. But how well? Of course, Stacey knew their families had been friends for years, but what she did not know was what kind of relationship had existed between the two of them apart from that.

The ringing of her phone jolted Stacey and she went to answer it, her mind still occupied with the disturbing encounter with Trish. She was so distracted that she did not recognize Kim's voice at first.

"I thought you said you were coming down right after Christmas!" Her friend's accusatory tone brought Stacey back to alertness.

All at once it seemed like a very good idea to go to San Francisco right away. It would be the best thing she could do. She needed to get away from Woodfern, away from Scott, and gain a better perspective on things. She had been too engrossed in what was happening, too caught up in the newness of her feelings about him. It would be easy to mistake them for something that was not real. Impulsively she told Kim she would come that weekend.

That was just two days away. As Stacey hung up, she knew she had much to do before she could leave on such short notice. But once the decision was made, her adrenalin began to flow and she started making preparations immediately.

She called Nora, who assured her she would mind the store by checking by the house every day or so while Stacey was gone, and that Brendan would be beside himself with joy to have Trinket to play with, so they would be glad to keep her little dog for her. Stacey thanked her and told her she would bring Trinket over the night before she left for the city.

The next day she took her car into town to be filled and checked before the trip. As she pulled into the service station she saw, with a little catch in her heart, that Scott's black sports car was up on the rack.

Ted Barnes, the owner mechanic, saw her as she drove up and smiled as he came toward her wiping his hands on a grease-blackened rag.

"That's a real little beauty," he said, jerking his head toward the Maserati. "Getting it tuned up for Scott. He's driving to the city Saturday."

So! Trish had been telling the truth. They were going to San Francisco together for the weekend. Instant dejection washed over Stacey. She had hoped Trish's words had just been a fabrication for her benefit.

"Now, what can I do for you, Miss Thornton?" Ted asked.

She had him fill her tank and check the oil, tires, and battery. That done, she started down Main Street just in time to see Scott, with Trish's arm tucked into his, enter Franklin's Jewelry Store.

Stacey accelerated and sped through town and out Crescent Beach Road. She did not stop until she found herself sitting in her own driveway leaning on the steering wheel, her heart palpitating hard. What had they been doing? Looking for engagement rings? Franklin's carried some lovely estate jewelry. More importantly, what kind of game was Scott playing? There could be no mistaking his flattering attention since the Christmas cast party, but was there, as others had hinted, an ulterior motive?

It was good that she was getting away, she told herself firmly. She was too close to the situation here. She did not like the power Scott Lucas had so quickly gained over her emotions. Why should she react violently to seeing him with Trish unless . . .

The "unless" part of her feelings she did not want to deal with at the moment. Instead, she would leave first thing in the morning, a day earlier than she had planned. She would take Trinket, with dog food, bed, and toys, down to Nora's this afternoon and then get an early start the next day.

As she drove over to the Phillips's Stacey remembered that she had doubted the truthfulness of Trish's insinuations. Now she was more inclined to believe them. She thought of the verse in John's Gospel: "You shall know the truth, and the truth shall make you free." Well, she had wanted to know the truth and now she was "free" — free of any illusions about Scott and of any possibility of a future with him. She was also free from the idea that he might have been the reason for her coming to Woodfern. She wasn't going to be foolish enough to think that anymore.

There was nobody at the house, so Stacey walked up to Jeff's pottery shack. He was busy at the wheel, and Stacey stood quietly watching him for a few minutes until he looked up. When he saw her, he smiled and lifted his foot off the pedal. "Hi, Stacey! Nora took Brendan and went shopping. She should be back soon."

"I'll wait then. I've decided to leave tomorrow so I brought Trinket. I hope that's O.K."

Jeff grinned. "Brendan's been talking of nothing else since Nora told him she was going to stay with us for a while."

"I appreciate it. I'll be staying with a friend and I'm not sure they allow pets in her building." Stacey hesitated, not knowing if Jeff was one of those temperamental artists who didn't like people watching them work. "Would you mind if I stayed up here and watched you for a little bit? It's absolutely fascinating."

"Of course not, Stacey. Stay!" He went back to shaping the pot he was making with his skillful hands while his foot kept the flywheel rotating with rhythmic precision. It seemed almost miraculous to Stacey that Jeff could take a lump of moist clay, envision a beautiful piece of pottery, and then with patience and talent create the object he had seen mentally.

As she silently watched his act of creation, repeated and confirmed by the other beautifully formed, glazed pieces finished on the shelves of the workshop, Stacey was reminded of a passage she had read in Isaiah only a few nights before: "O Lord. You are our Father; we are the clay, and You our potter; and all we are the work of Your hand." It seemed so significant to her just now. Just as Jeff took the raw clay, kneaded it like dough into a pliable mass by adding vinegar to it, then "threw" it on the potter's wheel, forming a useful and beautiful vessel from it, so God does with lives. Stacey pondered over the idea that sometimes a little "vinegar" mixed into people's experiences helped to make them more pliant in God's hands, more able to be formed to His likeness and into useful and beautiful vessels.

The identifiable blowing of the van's horn announced Nora's arrival back from the store. Stacey thanked Jeff and went to meet her friend. Brendan was already hugging Trinket around the neck, and the small dog was happily licking the little boy's rosy cheeks in return.

"Those two will be great pals," Nora assured Stacey. "Come on in."

"I can't stay long. I've decided to leave in the morning and I still have packing to do," Stacey told her but followed her into the cottage.

"You can have a cup of tea at least," Nora said, holding up the copper kettle Stacey had given her. "I really love this!"

"Oh, sure," Stacey said, sitting down in the

rocker with an unconscious sigh.

Nora gave her a quick look. "I've been dying for a good chat with you. I haven't really seen you for weeks. Not since Scott Lucas has been taking up all your time," she said with a wink.

"Oh, that!" Stacey sighed again.

Nora's eyes looked troubled, but she went on measuring tea into the teapot. Then she gave Stacey a concerned glance.

"Is everything O.K.? Is something wrong?"

"No, I mean yes." Stacey gave a half-laugh. "Everything is terrible. It couldn't be much worse," she said finally.

"About you and Scott?"

"It's over."

"It can't be!" Nora exclaimed.

Stacey nodded. "I have it on the best authority. He's probably going to marry Trish Findlay."

"He isn't!" gasped Nora. "How do you know?"

Briefly Stacey gave her a thumbnail sketch of her visit from Trish, then of seeing them in Woodfern going into the jeweler's and the confirmation by the garage mechanic that Scott's car was being readied for a trip.

Nora's eyes narrowed. "Did Trish actually say — ?"

"She didn't have to, not in so many words.

She didn't even try to be subtle. She made sure I got the message."

"What does Scott say about it? Did he confirm it?"

"He doesn't have to, Nora. Don't you see? He was only softening me up. He still wants the property."

"I don't believe it. I mean, I know he's interested in you," Nora said firmly. "I can tell."

"Interested in me? In my property you mean. I guess I had to learn the hard way that Scott has never given up his original intention of getting that land — by whatever means. Larry Meade and Leta Townsend tried to warn me. And they've both known Scott longer than either of us."

Nora was silent while she filled the teapot with boiling water, replaced the lid, and got out her best cups and saucers. She placed the jar of honey on the table and put some thin ginger cookies on a plate and set them alongside the flowered teapot. Then she sat down across from Stacey. "I don't believe it."

"You'd better. It's true." Stacey sighed. "It's probably the best thing all the way around. Scott Lucas is not the man for me. The sooner I accept that the better off I'll be."

"Is that the way you really feel? Or are you just playing it safe?"

The question caught Stacey off guard, and as she dipped the little wooden spooner into the golden honey, she realized she was not sure of the answer herself. But with more conviction than she felt, she said, "Of course."

Nora put both elbows on the table, balancing her tea cup delicately on the tips of her fingers, and raised one eyebrow. " 'Methinks the lady doth protest too much!' " she said softly.

"Oh, Nora! You're a romantic die-hard. I'm a realist," declared Stacey. "What I need is a good dose of the city. I've been secluded too long in a house that is full of memorabilia and romantic memories."

After leaving Nora's Stacey drove back into town and went to the post office. She wanted to tell Ellie Shannon, the postmistress, to hold her mail until her return. Aris Brady came in while she was talking to Ellie, so Stacey told her she was going to San Francisco.

"How long will you be gone?" Aris asked.

"I'm not sure. A week, ten days maybe," Stacey replied. "I need some rest and relaxation," she said with a laugh.

"Woodfern's going to be deserted! Fay's in Mexico and Shawn and Val left for New York. Well, be sure to let us know when you get back. We'll have a homecoming party!" Aris laughed. "At this time of the year I look for any excuse for a party to get me out of the doldrums. This weather!" She shook her head and they both laughed. It was then that Stacey noticed King Steele lurking in the shadows of the old building near the wall of metal post boxes. She wondered if he had come into town alone or if Scott was in the pickup outside. She could see its familiar yellow body with the unmistakable Lucas brand on the side. She did not know whether to linger a little longer chatting with Aris in order to avoid coming face-to-face with the surly foreman or to dash out the door while she had the chance.

She risked leaving, and a darting glance toward the pickup assured her Scott was not inside. She felt a mixture of relief and disappointment. But she knew she was not ready to see Scott yet.

As she was unlocking the front door, she could hear the phone ringing. She knew she couldn't make it in time to answer it, and by the time she reached her sitting room/office it had stopped ringing. It might have been Scott, and she really did not want to talk to him. She needed the space the trip would give her — the time to think things through and sift fact from fiction.

She finished her packing and set her alarm clock for six. The house seemed strangely lonely without Trinket's shadowing her everywhere. The scampering sound of her little paws up and down the stairway, or even her nerve-racking watchdog performance when the old house creaked or the wind loosened a shutter would have been welcome. She heard the rain start again as she settled down to sleep, and it was still drizzling the next morning when she locked the house and carried her suitcase out to the car. Her melancholy lingered as she drove past the Woodfern outskirts, over the bridge, and made the turn onto the freeway. It was not until she was just above Petaluma and the sun hit the rolling, oak-covered hills that Stacey's spirits began to lift.

Chapter Seventeen

As she neared the city Stacey felt the old excitement begin to stir. More than any other city in the world, San Francisco held a magic for her. It had the surface sophistication of Paris but not its ennui, the glitter of London without its tired dowdiness, the energy and sheen of Los Angeles without its phony glitz.

The tenseness she had felt in the flow of the traffic eased as she turned up the familiar hilly street where Kim's apartment, hidden behind a brick wall and an arched wooden gate, nestled between towering condominiums. Kim had always had fantastic luck, and finding this gem of an apartment had been one of her best "breaks." The rent was outrageous, but even when Kim complained about paying it, she knew it would be snapped up in a minute by envious friends who valued a prestigious address.

Kim ran an exclusive clothing boutique for an owner who had more money than taste and used the store as a tax shelter. For all intents and purposes it was Kim's store and reflected her personality and style. Her apartment, too, was decorated to suit the energy and vivaciousness of its tenant, and Stacey felt a warm flush of affection for her friend as she let herself in.

"Welcome, stranger!" read the note Kim had left on the front door. "I should be home around six. Make yourself at home. See you soon. Love, Kim."

In spite of her happy memories of the place, walking into Kim's living room was somewhat of a culture shock for Stacey. With its pale yellow walls, natural linen sofa, and bamboo armchairs cushioned in a splashy lemon and viridian green print, it was quite a contrast to the dark woods and deep-colored plush upholstery of the rooms she had been living in. Yellow tulips stood in vases on the coffee table and on the counter that divided the small, spare kitchen from the main living space. The whole atmosphere was one of spritely, urban charm.

True to her word, at six the door burst open and Kim arrived, her arms full of packages. With a shrill cry of greeting, she dumped her bags and gave Stacey a hug.

"Oh, how wonderful to see you! How long can you stay?" Her questions tumbled over each other. "Everyone is dying to see you but I told them you were mine exclusively, at least for the weekend! There's so much to talk about! So much I want to hear!"

Stacey had to laugh, not able to answer until Kim ran out of breath.

"I brought some goodies for dinner! All the San Francisco foods I'm sure you've been missing!" Kim began unpacking her purchases. "Voilà! The one, the only, the authentic San Francisco sourdough French bread!" She pulled along, golden brown, twisted loaf out of one sack and waved it like a flag. "We've got Bay shrimp, artichokes, mushrooms, and wild rice mix. But all that can wait till later," Kim finished with a flourish. Then she sighed. "Thank goodness it's Friday! What a week it's been! How was your trip? I bet you're bushed, too. Let's have a glass of wine and unwind!" suggested Kim, kicking off her high-heeled pumps and going toward the refrigerator.

"Not for me, Kim."

Kim turned with a bottle of white wine in one hand. "Still don't drink? I thought you'd have been driven to it by now, spending all this time in that place beyond nowhere where you've buried yourself." Kim's teasing smile exhibited two deep dimples on either side of her full, red mouth. "O.K. then. How about some herbal tea, guaranteed to rejuvenate the tired traveler?"

"Fine, that would be good," Stacey said, seating herself on one of the high stools in front of the counter. "You look marvelous, Kim," she commented.

"Thanks! I work at it," Kim said, laughing. "Well, I have to in my job. Customers are always checking me out to see what I have on. It sells merchandise. So, I guess I'm doing O.K."

When the tea was made they went over to the sofa where Kim collapsed and put her stockinged feet on the coffee table. Then she turned her "now tell all" gaze upon Stacey.

"Well, come on, who is he?" she demanded. "I know there's something more than a houseful of old furniture keeping you up in Woodfern."

Stacey shrugged. "It's a long story. Mind if I wait a while to fill you in on the details?" It was all still too near the surface to discuss even with as close a friend as Kim.

Kim did not persist. She was never at a loss for conversational subjects, and she immediately launched into an account of the latest happenings among their mutual friends in San Francisco. She talked all through dinner preparations, through the meal, and as they cleaned up the tiny kitchen together. Then, suppressing a yawn at midnight, Kim opted for bed.

"We've got loads of time to talk," she reminded Stacey sleepily.

Kim's sofa made up into a comfortable bed, and Stacey thought once she was settled into its downy depths she would fall asleep immediately. But in the absence of Kim's chatter, her thoughts rushed back to the uneasy ones she had been wrestling with before she left Woodfern and during the drive to the city. She could not stop thinking about Scott Lucas.

Finally she turned on Kim's TV, with the sound turned down and using earphones so as not to disturb her in the next room, but Stacey could not get interested in the late-night talk show. She kept seeing Scott's face superimposed on one of the guests who had a superficial resemblance to him.

Could she have been totally wrong about him?

She had almost convinced herself that Scott was sincere, open, and trustworthy, and that his feelings for her were becoming as strong as hers for him. When would she learn not to go by her feelings? They had too often betrayed her. As with Todd, she had been enticed by surface qualities. She had believed in Scott because she wanted to. *So much for woman's intuition,* she told herself scornfully.

"I should have learned from experience," she whispered miserably to herself. She could almost hear the words she had read in some article somewhere: "Know that using your head is as important as following your heart. A first unhappy romance can be chalked up to inexperience, a second to being caught off guard, but if you plunge into a third one without heeding the potential for unhappiness, then you are simply a fool!"

Still, with a tug of aching remembrance, Stacey thought of the night Scott had sung "If Ever I Should Leave You" to her, the times he had brought her a crimson rose, those special firelit hours, the first kiss . . . and the last one.

"Never again!" Stacey told herself grimly, dragging the pillow under her head, shifting her position on the couch, and staring at the TV screen. Suddenly she realized she had been watching the test pattern and, annoyed, switched the TV off. "Forget Scott Lucas," she ordered herself determinedly. She listened to the dim sound of the city traffic outside for a while and then finally fell asleep.

The days she spent with Kim were full, fun, and frenetic. They shopped endlessly at Ghiradelli Square, Imports on the Wharf, and Embarcadero complex; they talked endlessly while shopping, eating, and after they came back to the apartment exhausted.

On Monday Kim went back to work, and Stacey went over to the gallery to see Max, who begged her to come back.

"It's been crazy since you left. I've had three different people and none of them has worked out," he pleaded. She felt complimented but refused. Max's last words were, "Think about it."

She met Felix Stern, an old friend, for dinner one night without Kim. Felix, intelligent, sensitive, and enthusiastic, gave her a glimpse of what had once made the city life seem so exciting. His homely featured face was alive with interest as he discussed the things he cared deeply about: music, art, and the films and documentaries he helped cut and edit.

"They're giving me a bigger budget this year, Stacey. I need an assistant. Why not come back and go to work with me?"

Again Stacey felt the pull, but there was something else stronger that made her smile, shake her head, and say, "I've got a business of my own now, you know, Felix."

He smiled and swirled the drink in his glass, watching it glitter in the candle glow. "Maybe you'll change your mind," he said.

Stacey roamed the city, visiting the Palace of Fine Arts and the Museum of Modern Art, riding the cable cars like a tourist, and attending a show at the planetarium in Golden Gate Park.

The following Saturday, she and Kim drove to Sausalito to have lunch at one of the restaurants that had been a favorite when Stacey lived there. It was a gloriously sunny day, warm for the first of February, and they sat outside at a table with an umbrella on a deck that was abloom with bright geraniums in wooden planters. They ordered mushroom quiche and spinach salad and, throwing caution and diets to the wind, quenched their hunger on the ever-present basket of French sourdough bread and butter.

Enjoying the sunshine and the relaxed atmosphere, Stacey was suddenly alerted by Kim's quick intake of breath and murmured "Uh-oh!" Then she whispered to Stacey, "Don't look now. Don't dare turn your head! Uh-oh! It's too late. He's seen us. He's heading this way."

Stacey's curiosity overcame her caution and she looked in the direction Kim had warned her not to, just in time to see Todd moving between the tables toward them.

In one fleeting impression, Stacey saw he had at last acquired the total San Francisco "young executive" look he had strived for. There was something else about him, too, that she had never noticed when she was going out with him, the swagger in his walk.

"Stacey!" He greeted her so effusively she was embarrassed to see several heads at the next table turn to look at them. "When did you get into town? And why —" he shook his finger at her playfully and demanded, "didn't you let anyone know you were leaving or where to get in touch with you?"

"She *did,* that is to a few *close* friends," Kim said sweetly.

Todd ignored the jibe and looked at Stacey, "I really tried, but nobody seemed to know your address."

"Did you try the gallery?" Stacey asked. "Max knew."

Todd shrugged. "Oh, Max! He was very cool to me. I don't think he ever liked me." He gave a depreciating laugh. "I think he was interested in you himself and rather resented me."

"Oh, for pete's sake, Todd!" groaned Kim, rolling her eyes.

He threw her an annoyed glance and went on talking to Stacey. "You're looking absolutely fantastic, Stacey. Country life must agree with you." He put his hand on the back of one of the chairs as if to pull it out, asking almost as an afterthought, "Mind if I join you?"

"Yes," said Kim bluntly.

Todd was taken aback and looked quickly to Stacey for a retraction. In another flash of memory, Stacey recalled all the broken dates, lame excuses, and transparent lies Todd had given her toward the end of their relationship, and hardened her own soft heart. He was, after all, intruding. Before she weakened and let him sit down, Stacey also remembered a night when she had counted on him as an escort and he had phoned her forty minutes before he was supposed to be there to tell her he had to work. Later she had found out he had accepted a last-minute invitation to fill in for a guest who had cancelled out on his boss's wife's dinner party.

"I'm sorry, Todd," Stacey explained. "Kim and I haven't seen each other in ages. You understand, I'm sure. Girl talk and catching up, you know."

Todd's face flushed, and he glanced uncertainly from one to the other. Kim never met his eyes and did not apologize. Finally he spoke directly to Stacey.

"I'd certainly like to see you while you're in the city, Stacey —"

She shook her head. "Sorry, Todd, that won't be possible."

He looked baffled. "But I'd really like to take you out to dinner. Somewhere special?" His voice trailed off bewilderedly.

"Thanks, but no thanks, Todd," Stacey said evenly, surprised that she felt no resentment or bitterness, just a kind of relief that they were no longer involved and that she would not have to spend another hour listening to Todd talk about himself.

When he had said an awkward good-bye and walked away, Kim gave a nod of satisfaction. "Congratulations! I wasn't sure you would do it, Stacey. You've always let people take advantage of you!"

"I'm learning!" Stacey replied enigmatically and opened the large menu so Kim could not read the expression on her face. Did she always let people take advantage of her? Had she done the same with Scott?

That night she finally told Kim about Scott. Her friend listened sympathetically without commenting until Stacey described the last encounter with Trish Findlay. When Stacey had finished, Kim announced, "I don't know if it's the answer, but I know what will help! Some new clothes! Come down to the boutique with me on Monday and try some on. We've got some wonderful buys on sale. Clearance to make room for our spring things. But they'll be great for the kind of weather you have up in that country!"

Kim was nothing if not pragmatic, Stacey thought. And she had to agree that it was fun trying on some of the luxury clothes in the store, even the ones not on sale.

On Monday morning she went in early with Kim before the store opened, and they had a great time trying on outfits with accessories that sometimes cost as much or even more than the dress.

Stacey did splurge on a feather-light, mohair, seafoam cape that would be perfect for misty nights in Woodfern and an apricot velvet dress that she had no clear idea when she would wear but could not resist. When she left the shop, she had to admit she did feel better. Promising to meet Kim for lunch, Stacey decided to take in an exhibit of French Impressionists Max had recommended. It was only to be in the city for a limited time.

Stacey picked up a catalogue at the entrance of the gallery and proceeded to wander through the well-lighted rooms where the paintings of some of her favorite artists were displayed. "A Day in the Country" was the name of the exhibition, and each picture depicted a rural French countryside scene, often with groups of people picnicking, boating, dancing, or enjoying a leisurely meal in an outdoor cafe. They were fresh, sparkling with color, spontaneous, and endearingly naive.

These artists were considered modern in

their day, Stacey recalled, but now their works seemed quaint and picturesque. They celebrated the simple life of kitchen gardens, flowering apple trees, rosy children, and happy adults. They drew the viewer into the picture so that one longed to linger in the sunshine, hold on to the moment that was as ephemeral as a summer afternoon. Somehow the artists had given posterity the gift of making that moment last forever.

Looking at the worlds Manet, Renoir, and Pissarro had created from their own trips into the country around Paris, Stacey was impressed with the similarity of those landscapes to the view from the hillside above Woodfern. Only a few months ago she had stopped her car and gazed at the town from a distance, thinking at the time that it resembled a French village. Now, looking at an artist's composition of a real French landscape, she felt a tug of longing, a kind of homesickness for Woodfern!

Scott had said almost the same thing to her about traveling in France — something about having the same kind of reaction, about the villages making him long for home.

Stacey tried to brush the memory away. She did not want to think about Scott. She tried to concentrate as she moved from room to room of the exhibit, studying the paintings and reading the brochure; she tried not to remember.

When she met Kim for lunch, her friend told her Felix had tried to reach her at the apartment and, getting no answer, had called the store. He was getting a party together for tonight of some of Stacey's old friends. They were to have dinner at a new Japanese restaurant, then go on to hear some music at one of the old haunts in North Beach.

Stacey felt a curious reluctance about the evening ahead but could hardly refuse when Felix had gone to all the trouble of planning and calling others to meet them.

But after dinner, when they were all crowded into a corner table of a dark little place, Stacey realized suddenly with a sense of déjà vu that this was like a hundred other nights she had known when she lived in the city. It was part of the singles scene, the same as night life in any big city. She recognized it all, the monotonous beat of the band playing raucous music, too many people, too many drinks, too little air.

She thought of her friends in Woodfern, of the sweetness of their fellowship, the mellow strum of Jeff's guitar when they sang songs around the fireplace at Nora's. All at once she longed fiercely to be there. She knew in her heart that she did not belong here in this

stuffy, smoke-filled atmosphere with the banal remarks and tired "come-on" glances, at least, not anymore.

Her head began to throb. Desperately she needed to escape. She grabbed her purse, murmured a whispered excuse to Kim, and headed for the exit. She knew someone would bring Kim home when she was ready to leave.

Lying wakeful on Kim's couch, she stared at the luminous dial of her travel clock. What was the matter with her? The city had always held a magic for her. Now everything seemed stale. Woodfern had spoiled the city for her. Crazy as that sounded, Stacey knew it was true. In Woodfern she had been freed from her old restless seeking after happiness, love, and a satisfactory lifestyle because she had found it there.

With or without Scott Lucas, Woodfern had become familiar and precious to her. She would leave in the morning, she decided. She would tell Kim when she got up to dress for work.

As soon as she had made the decision, Stacey flipped her pillow over, curled up, and went soundly to sleep.

Chapter Eighteen

The usual morning fog had covered San Francisco when she left, but it lifted above Santa Rosa and the sun broke through the overcast. Early signs of spring could be seen in the countryside Stacey was now driving through. There was little traffic, and she should reach Woodfern before dark. She had asked Kim to call Nora when she got to work so Nora would be expecting her back.

She stopped in Cloverdale for lunch and browsed in an interesting antique and second-hand bookstore near the restaurant. By the time she started driving again, the weather had changed subtly. Some time later she began to run into a misty rain.

The farther north she drove the heavier the mist, until she was running into some thick patches of fog. With still more than a hundred miles to drive, it looked as though it was going to be a slow, tedious trip.

It was then she saw the road sign for

Mendocino and remembered Florin's recommendation of it as a "must see." Maybe if she detoured for a stop there the weather might clear and she could take the coastal route to Woodfern. The weather on the north coast was erratic, as Stacey had learned. Sometimes storms and sunshine were interchangeable and quickly moved from one to the other. An hour or two in Mendocino was not going to make that much difference to her arrival time in Woodfern.

Later Stacey wondered if the decision had been impulse or destiny. But at the time she just took the exit and within minutes found herself in a little town that seemed even more like New England in character than Woodfern. Situated on craggy headlands, Mendocino ambled up and down hilly streets, a conglomeration of weathered Victorian buildings that seemed to combine the aura of an early Western frontier town as well.

She easily found a parking space since the tourist season was over. The place seemed to have regained the quiet somnolence of the days when only a handful of Portuguese fishermen, a few farmers, and lumberjacks walked the boarded sidewalks.

Drawn by the beautiful displays of rare china pieces in the window of a corner shop, Stacey turned to go inside when she was startled to hear her name called.

"Stacey!"

She froze, her hand on the door handle. There was no mistaking that voice.

"Stacey!" It came again, this time closer.

She turned to see Scott striding toward her, a broad smile on his face. "What unbelievable luck!" he said. "What are you doing in Mendocino?"

"I could ask you the same thing," she stammered. Over his shoulder she saw his black sports car parked across the street. It was empty. That didn't mean Trish Findlay wasn't with him. Perhaps she was shopping in one of the many intriguing shops.

"Where have you been for the last week?" Scott asked her. "I called and then went by, but found the house closed. No sign of you. Why didn't you let me know you were going to be out of town?" He frowned at her fiercely. "Never mind, I can hear all about it over a cup of coffee." He took her arm and started leading her back across the street.

Stacey's first impulse was to run. She did not want to see Scott — not this way — with her guard down, unprepared. She had wanted to be cool, composed, and indifferent when she saw him again. But now it was too late. In spite of her mental rehearsal of what she would say and how she would act when she saw Scott again, the excitement she felt being near him wiped all the neat phrases she had thought up completely out of her mind.

The next thing she knew they were seated in a wooden booth in a little bakery and coffee shop and Scott had ordered coffee and apple crumb cake for both of them.

"Now, some explanations, young lady. Why did you leave town as if the sheriff and his posse were after you?" he said accusingly.

She looked over at him and saw something in his face that both frightened and thrilled her, something she had never expected to see in Scott Lucas's eyes. They were gazing at her in a kind of tender amusement but with something else, more important, that she dared not name.

She answered his question with a question. "Are you alone?"

He scowled. "Alone? What do you mean, alone? Yes, I'm alone. I'm on my way to San Francisco to catch a plane to New York. I couldn't bring Troy with me on this trip."

"New York?" she echoed.

"Yes, I'm going to visit the llama preserve in the Catskills," he told her. "With the weather so bad up our way, planes have been canceling flights, so I thought it was a better idea to drive to San Francisco, leave my car there, and fly out from International Airport."

He reached across the table and placed his hands over her clasped ones. "So, you see, it was just pure luck — or fate — that we met here. We could have passed each other on the divided freeway and never known. Like two ships passing in the night, right?"

Or divine coincidence? Stacey's mind suggested. Her heart began to pound, and although she started to pull away her hands, he held them fast.

"It's incredible luck!" he repeated. "I've missed you. Don't ever do that again. Don't leave without telling me."

Slowly she drew her hands out from under his and, trying to appear nonchalant, asked, "What possible difference could it make to you one way or the other if I'm out of town, Scott?"

He looked at her, head to one side. "Seriously? You don't know why?"

She shook her head, stirring sugar into her coffee.

"I thought I'd made that fairly clear," he said.

She spooned more sugar into her cup. "What about Trish Findlay?" she blurted out, scooping up another spoonful of sugar. She felt hard fingers on her wrist.

"Whoa! You're going to get a carbohydrate high! I thought you only used one spoonful of sugar per cup." Scott scowled at her. "What do you mean, 'What about Trish'?"

"I had the impression you two — I mean, aren't you engaged to be married?"

"Married!" Scott set his coffee mug down with a bang. *"Me?* Marry *Trish?* You've got to be kidding! What ever gave you such a crazy idea?"

Stacey took a sip of her coffee, then made a face. It was sickeningly sweet. She put it down.

"Tell me. Where did you get that kind of impression?" Scott persisted.

"I just thought. Well, she was in the shop and told me . . . at least, that's what I got from what she said." Stacey halted, flustered. "She was looking at china, and then she said you ought to help her pick it out. Then she said something about a wedding and that you were going to drive to San Francisco and maybe you would find something there you both liked. And then, I saw you two go into Franklin's Jewelry Store and I assumed —"

"You assumed wrong. Look, Stacey, maybe it would have been easy for you to get such an impression from what Trish said. I don't know. I did drive her to San Francisco last weekend, actually to Mann. Mainly because her parents didn't want her to drive by herself. And because I was invited to the same wedding. It was Trish's cousin's wedding. That's what she was talking about; I had asked her to help me pick a wedding present because I thought she would know more what her cousin might want or need. Does that clear up the mystery?"

Relief made Stacey feel suddenly weak. There was no point in telling Scott that Trish had purposely given her the wrong impresssion. In fact, such an explanation went totally out of Stacey's head at Scott's next words.

"And if I were considering marriage, Trish Findlay would hardly be the one. She's too young, too immature, too spoiled, too shallow —" he broke off. "Don't you want another cup of coffee? It seems to me you've ruined that one." He picked up her mug and took it over to the counter and waited while the cheerful waitress refilled it with fresh coffee from the urn.

He brought it back and put it down in front of Stacey. "Are you planning on going back to Woodfern tonight?" he asked.

"Yes."

"Well, I don't think you should. The fog was getting thicker even as I drove here. It would be really treacherous by the time you got back onto the freeway again. It's a hazard driving in it. I suggest you stay here overnight

250

and start back tomorrow. That would be much safer." He smiled. "We could have dinner and spend the whole evening together. I was going to try to make it a little farther, but —" and he threw up his hands and shrugged. "Why fight fate?"

Stacey hesitated. Hadn't she warned herself to follow her head and not just her heart?

"It really is the best thing to do," he said. Caring and concern were in his eyes as well as that elusive something else she had seen earlier. And Stacey wanted to find out what it was.

"I guess you're right," she said slowly.

Scott grinned mischievously. "Of course. I know I am."

At this time of year, reserving a room at the Mendocino Inn was no problem. When the bellhop opened the door for her, Stacey noted immediately that the massive Victorian bed, the dresser, and the mirror were authentic antiques. Scott had suggested they dine at the Inn, and Stacey was happy that Kim had persuaded her to buy the lovely apricot velvet dress. Suddenly she had been given the perfect opportunity to wear it.

She fixed her hair in a loose, "Gibson girl" knot, allowing a few strands that had curled in the damp air to fall in tendrils about her ears. Then she fastened in the amber cameo earrings she had discovered among some of Aunt Eustacia's jewelry and saw that they might have been chosen especially for the dress.

The rich hues of the dress deepened the brown of her eyes and complemented the glowing color of her skin. Her own critical, last-minute check in the mirror before descending the stairs to meet Scott did not see what his eyes saw, however. Stacey was completely unaware of the heightened sparkle and radiance only love can give a woman.

They sat in the deep wing chairs drawn up in front of the fireplace at one end of the long living room that adjoined the dining room. Their eyes met and they smiled while a waiter took their orders.

"You look like you belong in this setting," Scott told her when the waiter had left. "There's something so old-fashioned about you. I mean that in the best possible way. It's like a hallmark on fine porcelain or sterling or some . . . precious gemstone."

Stacey felt her face flush and she lowered her eyes. "You make me sound like an antique!" she said lightly to offset how his remark had touched her.

"If that means rare, one-of-a-kind, and special, I guess that's what I meant," Scott agreed, his eyes resting on her as he laughed gently.

The waiter came back with a tray bearing ice-filled glasses and two small bottles of Perrier. Scott and Stacey were silent as he poured the French mineral water into the glasses, added a twist of lime, and handed them each a glass with a small, lace-edged, linen napkin.

"I still can't get over the luck of meeting you here," Scott said, shaking his head a little. "The chances are about one-in-a-million, you know."

Again Stacey's heart gave a small lurch of recognition. *It's true,* it seemed to be telling her. This meeting was not by chance.

They fell silent again and the firelight played on their faces as they stared into it, each with secret thoughts. Then simultaneously they spoke.

"I wanted to tell you —" began Stacey.

"I tried to —" Scott started to say.

They both stopped, laughing.

"Go on," Scott said.

"You first," Stacey urged.

"It was just that when I couldn't reach you by phone, I felt so — I don't know. Then when I drove by the house and saw it all dark and empty . . . it was almost as if you had never come and lived there or . . . and I felt terribly upset by that." He took a sip of his drink, then went on. "I guess it was then I began to realize how it was before I met you. And how lost I felt without you."

Before Stacey could respond, their waiter reappeared to tell them their table was ready and the first course was served.

Their cream of fresh mushroom soup was hot and delicious, the entree of red snapper broiled to perfection, the rice pilaf and broccoli hollandaise equally well prepared.

Through the door of the dining room they could see into the cocktail lounge where a folk singer, a pretty, long-haired young woman was sitting on a stool and singing plaintively to the accompaniment of her guitar.

"Do you like folk music?" Scott asked.

"Some, yes," Stacey replied.

"Why, I wonder, are the 'folk' always so sad?" asked Scott quizzically.

Stacey laughed. "I know what you mean. But I think it's mostly when Americans sing folk music that they sound like that. In Europe, some of the folk music is very gay — riotous, even — especially the Irish and Basque."

This launched them into more reminiscences about their experiences in Europe, and by the time they finished swapping stories the waiter was back asking them if they cared for dessert.

They declined.

"Would you like to go in and listen to her music for a while?" Scott asked Stacey as they rose from the table. "Or would you rather have coffee in front of the fire . . . at *our* place?"

"That sounds nicer."

He took her hand as they walked back into the nearly deserted living room and found the wing chairs empty and waiting.

"Are you glad you took my advice and stayed over?"

She nodded, "Yes, very."

"You know, when we were speaking earlier about marriage," Scott said slowly, "I was surprised that you would ever have thought I'd be interested in anyone like Trish, as a marriage partner, at least. I'm looking for so much more in a woman than Trish could ever possibly be."

"Maybe you're being unfair. She is very young. People change. I've changed, I know, even since I came to Woodfern. This past week in the city, among the friends I used to know, doing the things I used to think were fun . . . well, they just don't appeal to me anymore."

"Do you know what you want now?"

"Well, not everything. But, I think I've got my priorities in better perspective."

"When I marry it's going to be forever. And

the person I marry will have to feel that way, too."

"I thought you were the cynic who believed love doesn't last!" Stacey said, gently teasing him.

"I guess that's what I've been afraid of, a love that wouldn't stand the test of time."

"Is that important to you?"

"I'd say it would be the most important consideration in my deciding whether to marry. I believe marriage is the most important step anyone takes, the most serious decision." He paused. "But you can't just set out with a list of qualifications and expect to find someone who meets them. There has to be the element of surprise — the romance — that's important to me, too."

"I wouldn't have guessed you were such an idealist."

"People have different sides to their personalities, once you get to know them. Or rather, when they let you get to know them. I'm careful to whom I reveal that part of me. I guess I've made a conscious effort to deny my vulnerability, maybe because I've been afraid to trust anyone enough to let them see me that closely." He paused, then reached over and took her hand, smoothing out each finger as it lay in the palm of his other hand. "That is — until now."

Stacey's heart leaped into her throat as she looked at him, into those eyes she once had thought so cold, which were now searching her with a kind of softness and . . . was it hope?

"I love you, Stacey," Scott said.

She drew in her breath. "But —" she protested faintly.

"Don't," he cautioned softly. "I'd given up. I really had. I'd let go all my early dreams of finding someone I could love forever, someone like you."

His words released something in Stacey. The feelings for this man that she had suppressed, tried to divert, deny, or argue away, suddenly came rushing to the surface with a tremendous sense of joy.

"So had I, Scott. Isn't it strange? I'd given up my dreams, too. I thought the kind of love I'd seen in my parents' marriage didn't exist anymore. Then, gradually, I began to hope again that it might be possible."

"I know." Scott nodded, smiling, his eyes shining with happiness. "I *know*. It just goes to prove that if two people are meant to meet and fall in love, then it happens. No matter what the odds seem to be, no matter what the bad beginnings! Nothing happens by chance. I believe that now."

Divine coincidence, Stacey's heart confirmed.

He walked her to the staircase when at last

they knew they had to say good night. Both of them would be leaving early in the morning with long drives ahead of them. At the foot of the steps in the now deserted lobby, Scott touched her cheek gently, then leaned over and kissed her, slowly, with deep sweetness.

She started up the stairs reluctantly. Then two steps above him she turned, and he put his arms on her waist. With her hands on his shoulders she leaned down and kissed him long and fully on his mouth. "Good night, Scott."

His arms tightened around her and he drew her closer. She heard him whisper her name and she felt the wonderful strength of his embrace. She sighed softly, full of wonder at what was happening. She had never really believed someone would care for her so sincerely and promise such fulfillment. Surely, it was the stuff dreams are made of, and her dreams seemed to be coming true.

Chapter Nineteen

Stacey could not remember her dreams when she woke up in the morning except that they had been vaguely pleasant and left her feeling euphoric.

A check of her wristwatch told her it was much later than she had planned to sleep. There were no phones in the rooms of the Mendocino Inn to receive a wake-up call. She dressed hurriedly and went downstairs. At the desk she was given a note from Scott.

"Good morning!" it said. "Sorry I had to leave before seeing you, but I had to get going to make my New York flight. As soon as I get home I'll be in touch. We have to make plans. Yours, Scott."

Scott certainly had not inherited his great-uncle Rollin's talent for writing love letters. Stacey was amused as she tucked the note into her handbag. How well Scott's tough exterior concealed his tender, sensitive, ideal-istic inner nature! His bold, distinctive handwriting told her a lot about him, though, she thought. There were unmistakable signs in it of a man who was confident, who knew what he wanted, and who would settle for nothing less.

Even though Stacey was disappointed at not seeing him before they went their separate ways, he had said he would be gone only a week, or ten days at the most. They would have lots of time to spend together when he got back.

Even now what had happened between them last night seemed unreal. "I'd given up finding someone like you." Scott's words replayed themselves thrillingly. The impossible had happened, and dreams did come true, after all.

She ate a hasty breakfast and was soon on the road. She felt as if she had been gone a long time from Woodfern and she was anxious to get home. She realized with delight that that was the way she thought of it now. Woodfern was *home.*

The sun sparkled on the sea as Stacey drove the winding coast road out of Mendocino to join the freeway north. The whitecaps danced in the sunlight, and gulls swooped down from the rocky cliffs above in a kind of orchestrated ballet. Stacey's heart was on tiptoe, her spirits bubbling. All the doubts and heaviness she had carried underneath the surface gaity of her city visit had magically lifted.

"It isn't Trish Findlay Scott Lucas loves, it's *me!*" she said out loud, laughing softly at the lovely surprise of it. Then as if on cue another song from *Camelot* came winging into her mind, and she broke into a joyous rendition of the exuberant "C'est Moi!"

She had no premonition, nothing to warn her, no presentiment of disaster as she entered Woodfern.

As she crossed over the graceful, arched bridge a lovely misty glow appeared on everything; the fields were yellow with mustard, the trees with the first delicate green of spring foliage. She turned off Main Street onto Crescent Beach Road feeling her anticipation rise as she headed homeward.

At the bend of the road she saw the house in the distance and the late afternoon sun reflecting on the tall, third-floor windows, making them bright as with an inner fire. It was startling, and unconsciously Stacey thought of Paul's recommending new wiring. "Old houses can be fire-traps; a short or something could set it off like a tinder box when a match drops on it," he had said. She would see about having it done right away, she decided.

As she neared the house, Stacey was amazed to see an unusual number of cars lined up along the side of the road. Then with a sickening sensation she saw a fire truck and several yellow-slickered firemen moving about in the driveway.

She braked joltingly, and her palms, suddenly sweaty, gripped the steering wheel convulsively. She stared at the scene in shock, trying to register the cause of the noise and confusion before her. Then she rolled down the car window and looked out. It was only then the acrid stench of smoldering wood and scorching smoke reached her nostrils.

She put the car quickly in gear and inched farther down the road, swerved to the right behind a pickup, the last vehicle parked along the drainage ditch, unbuckled her seat belt, and with shaking hands pushed open the car door and got out. Knees trembling, she half-ran, half-stumbled toward the driveway.

When she reached it one of the firemen, a man she did not recognize, halted her. "Sorry, ma'am, nobody's allowed —"

"But this is my property! I'm Stacey Thornton, the owner. What happened?" she asked in a quavering voice.

The man's expression altered. He shook his head. "I'm sorry, ma'am. We don't know yet the extent of the damage —"

A quick look beyond his towering bulk assured her that the house was intact. Then her frantic gaze went past him to the side, and she saw that it was the barn on which two firemen were aiming their huge hose.

Stacey stiffened, thinking of all the things stored inside the now-blackened, crumbling structure.

"How did it start?" she asked through stiff lips. But before the fireman could answer, Stacey heard her name called and turned to see Nora running toward her with tears streaming down her face.

The whole scene was like a nightmare, and afterward Stacey could not remember clearly what happened in the next few hours. She recalled seeing Nora's dirt- and tear-streaked face, her wild hair, and her distressed eyes, as she held out her arms. They hugged, holding on to each other as Nora stammered out words that at first Stacey could make no sense of. Nora kept saying, "Oh, Stacey, I'm so sorry, so sorry! If it hadn't been for Paul and Jan . . . it might not even have been discovered until too late! They saw the blaze and called the fire department immediately, and Paul started dragging things out himself until the blaze got too hot. But the wood was so old and all that furniture!" she wailed.

"Thank God, at least no one was hurt!" Stacey gasped.

"Yes! But that's not all, Stacey. Trinket's

gone!" she sobbed. "Kim called me from San Francisco yesterday morning, and when you didn't come last night I thought you'd been stopped somewhere by the fog. I was coming here this morning to bring Trinket back and to get things ready for you . . . and as I drove up the fire was really — I mean, the flames were coming up through the loft part of the barn and the fire trucks were tearing down the road! I was so shocked and scared. I wasn't thinking. I jumped out of the van and started running with some idea that I could help some way, I guess. I saw Paul and Jan, and then the firemen came and . . ." she broke off. "I'm afraid Trinket must have gotten out of the van and maybe was frightened by all this and ran away!"

Stacey clung to Nora as the new shock waves hit her and tried to comfort her as best she could. She felt as if she had turned to stone.

"At least no one was hurt," she kept repeating. "It could have been worse."

Over Nora's shaking shoulders she saw Paul and Jan coming slowly toward her, their faces sad, eyes red-rimmed.

"Sorry, Stacey. We did the best we could . . . We got some of the stuff out. I don't know what's in the barrels but — we were coming over to get the bedroom suite you said we could have. Thank God, we came when we did. It's not a total loss . . ."

The third morning after the fire Stacey sat at her desk with a pile of insurance forms in front of her waiting to be filled out, but she stared, immobile, out the window at the scarred wreck of the barn.

The loss of a few priceless antiques seemed minimal in comparison to the loss of her little canine companion. She missed Trinket more than she thought possible. Trinket had been part of her life for the last two years — an intrinsic part, she was discovering, without which she felt bereft. Trinket had been there to greet her every evening when she had come home from work in the city, had seemed to know when Stacey felt low or happy, lonely or glad. She had traveled well, fiercely protected, and proudly possessed Stacey. Stacey could not get used to her not being there.

Nora had been repentant and inconsolable.

"I should never have left her! I just acted instinctively and I must have left the van door open!"

Stacey tried to console her friend by saying, "She may come back. Dogs do find their way home even when they've been lost a long time. You're always seeing newspaper stories about that kind of thing."

But in her heart Stacey doubted it. Trinket was a city dog. If she had been frightened by the calamitous fire, the noise of the fire engine, the shouts and loud noises, she probably had taken off into the woods. Stacey was not at all sure she would not have been hurt or even killed there by predators such as coyotes or a bobcat. Trinket had not even been allowed out in the yard without her collar attached to a sliding hook on a wire that stretched between two trees.

Stacey remembered one day when she was going shopping with Nora and she had put Trinket out on the utility porch before leaving. Nora had asked, "Won't she be all right in the yard?"

"She might somehow get loose from the chain and try to run after us and get hit by a car. Trinket's a city dog," she had explained.

"Wouldn't she eventually adjust?" Nora had replied, adding teasingly, "You're a city girl and you've adjusted."

Stacey had laughed a bit ruefully. "Not easily."

Now the words came back to haunt her.

The sound of car tires on the driveway outside brought Stacey back from her sad reminiscing. She got up from her desk and started toward the front of the house just as Larry Meade gave the doorbell a twist. His usual grin was missing. Instead, he looked tight-lipped and grim.

"Why, Larry, hello. This is a welcome visit, I was feeling pretty gloomy. Maybe you can cheer me up," Stacey said.

Larry stepped inside. "I'm afraid not, Stacey. In fact, I'm afraid I'm the bearer of bad tidings."

"More? I thought I'd had my quota!" Stacey exclaimed.

"It's about the fire."

"Yes?"

"There's going to be an investigation as to its cause."

Something in Larry's expression started an uneasy staccato in her heartbeat.

"We believe . . . it was deliberately set. We've found evidence of arson," he said solemnly.

"We?" Stacey questioned in a puzzled voice.

"The Volunteer Fire Department committee that investigates fires."

Stacey had forgotten Larry was a member of the local VFD. "Arson is an ugly word," she repeated distastefully.

"It's a crime."

"But who would do such a thing?" She shook her head dazedly. "I mean, isn't it usually a form of fraud . . . or for monetary gain or simply the work of a firebug?"

"It could be any of those or it could be an act of misplaced loyalty," Larry said sternly.

"Loyalty?" Stacey frowned, not understanding.

"A grudge, revenge." Larry shrugged. "I hate to show you this, Stacey. But it seems irrefutable. We found oil cans discarded in the back of the barn, and among the ashes and rubble, this." He held out his hand, opening it, palm up.

Stacey looked at the metal button within it.

"Look closer," he directed.

She leaned forward, then picked it up. On its surface were the three initials LVR, interlocked in the logo of Lucas Valley Ranch.

"You don't mean — You can't think —" Stacey's stunned protest trailed away in the wake of Larry's steady, unwavering look of confirmation.

"But why? Who from Lucas Valley Ranch would — ?"

"Intimidation maybe. Scott Lucas did want your land. Maybe the only thing left was to scare you off."

Stacey's fingers clenched around the offending metal. Its edges cut into the soft skin of her palm as she lashed out, "No! I don't believe it! Scott wouldn't —"

"I didn't say Scott himself. He could have dropped a word here or there, or hinted

268

around the ranch his frustrations about not getting you to sell. One of the hands perhaps assumed his boss was giving an indirect order . . ." Larry let his words hang insinuatingly.

Stacey simply stood there shocked into silence.

Larry went on. "Scott's out of town. But as soon as he gets back there's going to be a full-fledged investigation. And we'll get to the bottom of this. Nobody, no matter who it is, will get away with arson."

After Larry left, Stacey moved through the house like a person in a hypnotic trance. All kinds of terrible thoughts assailed her, thoughts so horrible and devastating that she could hardly bear it. Could what Larry had said possibly be true? Had Scott in some way indicated something that was misinterpreted by one of his men? Had it even been planned with his knowledge?

"No! No!" She heard her voice, loud and emphatic, deny it.

Yet, little by little, as Stacey paced the length of the house and back, bits of random evidence to substantiate Larry's allegations began to take form, to thrust themselves accusingly into her consciousness. Both Scott and King Steele knew she was out of town. She remembered now seeing the ranch foreman in the post office when she had gone to tell them to hold her mail. He had probably overheard her telling Aris Brady she would be gone.

Scott couldn't have been involved, Stacey told herself determinedly. For whatever reason he himself had been in Mendocino, he couldn't have known she would be there. But, then, he had persuaded her not to drive back to Woodfern that day, hadn't he? If he knew the plot, might he not have purposely delayed her another day?

"No! I'll never believe he had anything to do with it!" she said out loud, stamping her foot in frustration. The man whose beautiful voice had thrilled her with hymns as well as with love songs, who had spoken sensitively of idealistic dreams and hopes, who had held her tenderly in his arms and told her he loved her, could not possibly have had a part in such a cruel, criminal action.

And yet, where had she read there was a dark side to everyone? Had Scott used her for his own ends? "Scott Lucas has a lust for land," Larry Meade had warned her months ago. Was it true? Had he used "love" as a means to an end? Had she somehow been tricked, lulled, betrayed again by someone?

It was hard to believe. But Stacey had to admit it was not altogether impossible. She would not have been the first woman to be duped by a man. It happened all the time. "How could she have been so dumb?" had been Stacey's usual reaction when she read some such account in the news. " 'I thought he loved me!' sobbed the heiress confronted with the evidence that her loving suitor had stolen her fortune and fled."

Somehow, Stacey began to feel just as stupid. Little by little all the magic of Mendocino began to seem like a farce played out for the sole purpose of deluding her.

She walked through the rooms, suddenly burdened by all these possessions, trapped in the house when all her instincts were to run, to leave Woodfern and all its painful associations. As she stood in the middle of one of the rooms her eyes lighted upon the last rose Scott had brought her. Since that first time, he had often brought her a single red rose. It had become a kind of symbol. She walked over to it and picked it up. The dried petals dropped to the floor. She had gone away, leaving it to wither in the crystal vase. With a half-sob, she threw the bare stem into the fireplace. It had been abandoned, rejected, just as she felt; part of the plot to be used, then tossed away. What a fool she was to have believed Scott Lucas!

Gripped with an anger that was hard and cold, her mind was cleared of self-pity.

Making a decision seemed imperative. Whatever the findings of the investigation turned out to be, she would not be there to receive them. There was no point staying in Woodfern any longer. All her hopes and dreams had been dashed to bits. Leaving seemed the only solution. The best thing for her to do would be to put Woodfern behind her forever.

It seemed to Stacey that within a matter of days she had lost everything she cared deeply about. Maybe her decision would be considered reckless, but she didn't care anymore. Once she had made up her mind, Stacey was adamant. She especially wanted to be gone before Scott returned from New York. The thought of facing him with what she now suspected was unbearable.

Perhaps it isn't rational, Stacey thought, keeping a running dialog with herself as she began to pack her personal belongings, *but I can't stay here. Not now.* She knew dealers who would buy the lot of antiques, and she would probably sell them at a loss. But even so, all she wanted was out, the sooner the better. Stacey was too strongly in the grip of emotions to think coolly.

Chapter Twenty

The next day her bags were packed and standing in the hall by the front door when Stacey saw Scott's yellow pickup speed into the driveway and stop with a squeal of brakes. She watched him jump out of its cab, letting the door swing shut, and march up to the house. Troy gave a couple of loud, protesting barks at being left in the back of the truck.

Stacey wanted to run. But it was too late. Scott was already striding for the front door.

Before he could knock, she opened the door, hastily gathering her inner resistance to anything he might say.

"What's this I hear about your leaving town?" he demanded, his words ringing harshly in her ears. They only served to stiffen her resolve not to be taken in by whatever arguments he put forth.

"It's true," she said shortly.

"How can you do that? Were you just going

to leave again without telling me? Without explaining?"

She lifted her head defiantly and retorted, "Aren't you the one who says 'Never explain; your friends don't need it and your enemies won't believe it'?"

"Don't play games with me, Stacey. I want some answers," he said angrily.

"I'd like some answers, too, Scott! Like who set fire to my barn!" Stacey flung back at him furiously, all her pent-up emotions surfacing at the sight of him and his arrogance. She started to walk away, but he caught her wrist, spinning her around to face him, his cool eyes flashing and his mouth hard and tense.

"I know about that rumor. But that isn't important right now. What's important is us! Have you forgotten that I love you?"

She felt herself losing control. How could he speak of love now? How dared he? She struggled to loosen his grip on her wrist, feeling the hot sting of tears rush into her eyes, and keeping her head averted so he wouldn't see them.

"I said I love you! Didn't you hear me?" His voice was low and intense. "Stacey!"

His hand tightened on her wrist. "Stacey, look at me!"

For a long moment there was absolute silence, tension so tangible, Stacey knew it had to snap or explode. Slowly she turned her head. Scott's eyes burned into hers.

"You want the truth? So do I. You can't possibly believe I had anything to do with the fire. I have to hear that from you first before I say anything more. What I want from you is commitment. I need to know that you trust me. I love you. I want to marry you. But I have to know you want that same kind of commitment. If there's no trust, no commitment, then love is no more than a word."

Hope struggled with doubt in Stacey's mind. The stress of the last few days had wearied her. Even now she wondered if listening to what Scott had to say would make any difference. A kind of cynicism had crept into her once accepting nature. As Kim said, she had been taken advantage of once too often.

"It really doesn't matter anymore, Scott. Someone or other wants me out of here badly enough to use any means. This is the worst, of course, but there've been other things . . ." She passed her hand across her forehead, pushing back a straying stand of hair. "You asked me once what a city girl was doing in this remote spot trying to run an antique business. Well, maybe you were right. Maybe I don't transplant so easily."

Scott's angry expression changed to one of

surprise and pain. "O.K.! Maybe I'm asking too much after what you've been through. Maybe I do owe you an explanation. I don't blame you." He continued with a kind of sad resignation in his voice.

"Larry Meade told me what they'd found after the fire. I questioned all my men. All denied any knowledge of it. But —" Scott sighed heavily, "King Steele has disappeared. King's had lots of problems over the years. Alcohol, mainly. He's got a mean temper and an unforgiving nature. He'll hold a grudge for no apparent reason." Scott shook his head. "King practically grew up on the ranch. He came here as a boy of fifteen. His father was a drifter and abused him badly. My dad took him on as a hand. He was about the same age as my older brother Dan, and they palled around together, hunting, fishing, and riding. King had an old back injury, something wrong with his vertebrae that was probably the result of some of the beatings he took as a child. Anyway, it prevented him from going into the service when Dan did. When Dan was killed King nearly went under. He disappeared then for a couple of years. My dad eventually found him in Marysville on skid row, brought him back to the ranch, and got him straightened out for a time, although he had periodic bouts with liquor. He had a fierce and jealous loyalty to my father after that. It became distorted. Like with this. . . . He must have gotten drunk — I really can't explain it. He was a bitter, hard guy. He took things as personal affronts, felt the world was against him." Scott halted. "Not that this excuses what he did but it may explain it. I told Larry that if you did decide to press charges or they could find more conclusive evidence, enough to bring him to trial. . . . I don't know if they can find him. Of course, I blame myself. He must have heard me talk about the extra pastureland and wanting to buy this property and just taken it upon himself to harass you."

Stacey remembered the nights she thought she had heard a prowler, the time the mailbox was knocked down, and other similar incidents that she had just chalked up to chance. They could all have been King's doings.

"If I've misjudged you, Scott, I apologize. But it's too late. I think I made a mistake coming here. Just like you once said, I'm a city girl and maybe neither my poor little dog nor I belonged here —"

"You're wrong, Stacey!" Scott interrupted vehemently. "You do belong here." His voice roughened. "I couldn't be wrong about you. I know you want the same kind of life I do, the kind we could have together — here in

Woodfern, a place I love and you've come to love. I know we share the same faith, the same values. Everything I've learned about you in the last several weeks makes me sure of that. So why are you leaving?

"If you walk out of my life now I'll have lost something infinitely precious and important. I thought you were the person God meant for me to share my life with. I can't believe He brought you into my life only to let me lose you."

Completely overwhelmed, Stacey looked at Scott. Did he really believe what he was saying? Why had he waited so long to say it?

He moved as if to take her in his arms, but she stepped away, warding him off, shaking her head. "No, Scott. It was a mistake. We could never —"

"Didn't you hear anything I was saying?" His voice became urgent and frustrated. "What do I have to do to convince you?"

Before she could reply they heard frantic barking outside and the reverberating sound of a dog's paws pounding repeatedly against the front door.

"What in the world?" Scott mumbled with a frown and strode over to the front door and yanked it open. His big black Lab ran to the edge of the porch still barking, then bounded back, jumping up on Scott, then running back to the steps, quivering with excitement.

"What is it, Troy? I told you to stay in the truck. Is something wrong?" The dog continued to bark and rush back and forth between Scott and the steps.

Scott turned around to Stacey, who had followed him to the door. "He's on to something," Scott told Stacey. "He wants me to go with him! Maybe it's an animal caught in a trap. Have you got a cat?" he asked.

"No, but Trinket is missing!" Scott ran down the porch steps. Troy was running full speed now, with Scott close behind. At the edge of the lawn they disappeared into the woods. Stacey grabbed her sweater and, flinging it around her shoulders, took off after them. She could hear the tone of Troy's bark change to one of triumph now that he had succeeded in getting his master to follow him.

They were far ahead of her when Stacey heard Scott shout something, and she increased her pace. Her feet slid on the slippery pine needles and sank into the muddy soil sodden with the weeks of winter rain. Then, as she came to a clearing, she picked up the sound of faint, pitiful whimpering. She saw Scott on his hands and knees with Troy standing beside him, his tail whipping, barking crazily.

"O.K.! O.K.!" Scott was saying soothingly

as Stacey came panting alongside.

"It's your dog," Scott explained. "She must have fallen through the rain-rotted boards covering this old well. I think I can lower myself down and get her," he said, and then proceeded to do so. Within a few minutes he emerged with a shivering, wet, miserable Trinket held firmly under his arm. Stacey pulled off her sweater and unfolded it like a blanket to receive the cold little dog into her open arms.

"I don't think she's injured," Scott said as they started back to the house with Troy prancing proudly ahead, then circling back, giving small barks as if he knew he'd accomplished something wonderful. "As soon as she's been fed and gets warm, she'll probably be fine."

Some time later, Trinket snuggled into her basket close to the kitchen wood stove, warm, fed, and worn out from her ordeal. Troy lay nearby, his massive head between his paws, basking in the praise of both his master and Stacey. He kept his eyes fixed on the object of his rescue.

"She's a rugged little creature after all," Scott commented with a smile. "City dog or not."

Stacey had made tea and was standing at the counter slicing a lemon. She turned and said quietly, "I'm so grateful to you and Troy for what you did today. I shudder to think I might have taken off never knowing Trinket was trapped in that old well. If you hadn't come today . . ." she broke off, shivering a little.

"I keep telling you it's fate. Everything that's happened to us could not all have been simply coincidence," Scott teased.

No? Stacey stood absolutely still. *Divine coincidence? Nothing happens by chance.* Her eyes wide with wonder, she stared at Scott so long that he got up from the kitchen table and came over to where she stood.

"What is it?" he asked. "You look so strange."

"I guess I just realized that maybe I do belong here after all."

"That's what I've been trying to tell you. You do belong here. Here in my arms. For always."

He kissed her gently at first, then with a swiftly deepening pressure. Stacey felt a rushing current of response in spite of herself. Yielding to it, she knew the sweetness of surrender. When the kiss ended, a smile trembled on her mouth. She laughed softly.

He looked at her puzzled. "What's funny?"

"I just remembered the law of community property in California. Everything a couple owns when they marry becomes joint property. So, you'll get your six acres after all!"

"That's hardly fair, is it?" Scott demanded with a frown. "I'll get a measly six acres and you get a sixty-acre ranch!"

Stacey put her head on his shoulder and closed her eyes blissfully, rejoicing in her heart with the words that now seemed confirmed in her love: "The lot is cast into the lap, but its every decision is from the Lord."